"How can you stay so upbeat and optimistic?"

From what Gabby had just told him, her thoughts, her attitude, should be just as dark, as pessimistic, as his were.

"I have to," she told him simply. "I have to believe that things do eventually work themselves out, that good triumphs over evil and that the sun will come up tomorrow," she concluded, the corners of her mouth curving as she deliberately quoted a lyric from an old favorite show tune.

A lyric that, as she could see by the man's totally unenlightened expression, was completely lost on Trevor.

But what wasn't lost on him was that, despite the partial darkness within the cab of the truck, Gabby seemed to glow.

And there was something very compelling about that.

Before he knew it, Trevor had decreased the space between them within the truck until there wasn't any—which was fine with him because he had no need of any.

At least not now, while he was kissing her.

The  **ve, high**

THE COLTON RANSOM

BY
MARIE FERRARELLA

First published in Great Britain 2013
by Mills & Boon, an imprint of Harlequin (UK) Limited,
Eton House, 18-24 Paradise Road, Richmond, Surrey TW9 1SR

© Harlequin Books S.A. 2013

Special thanks and acknowledgement to Marie Ferrarella for her contribution to The Coltons of Wyoming miniseries.

ISBN: 978 0 263 90720 9
ebook ISBN: 978 1 472 01250 0

18-0713

Marie Ferrarella, a *USA TODAY* bestselling and RITA® Award-winning author, has written more than two hundred books for Mills & Boon, some under the name Marie Nicole. Her romances are beloved by fans worldwide. Visit her website, www.marieferrarella.com.

To avid readers everywhere.
Where would we writers be
without you?

Prologue

A baby.

What the hell was he going to do with a baby? And a baby *girl,* to boot.

But boy or girl, one thing was a given. He didn't know the first thing about taking care of something so helpless, so dependent. Hell, he hadn't been taking care of anyone but himself for *years*. He had no idea how to *start* raising a kid, let alone an infant.

There had to be a way out of this. A way that, in the long run, would be better for the baby, not to mention better for him.

Almost two weeks into this so-called parenting thing and he still felt like a man who'd been pushed out of an airplane and was free-falling to earth without so much as a handkerchief to serve as a makeshift parachute.

Trevor Garth paced the floor in his bedroom as he stared at the crying infant he was holding in his arms. How could something so small make so much noise?

Or throw his entire heretofore orderly life on its ear?

At thirty-four, Trevor had assumed that his life would be winding down, settling into a predictable pattern. No more dodging bullets or chasing down armed criminals. That was one of the reasons he'd left the Cheyenne police force five years ago and taken this position as head of security here at Jethro Colton's Dead River Ranch. In his experience, nothing much of any consequence happened here as long as you steered clear of Jethro Colton when the old man was in a mood—which was often enough. But he was good at keeping under the radar, doing what needed to be done without calling any attention to himself.

Until now.

Trevor glared at the infant he couldn't seem to appease or soothe, despite his attempts to rock Avery to sleep.

This, he thought darkly, was what happened when he took a vacation. Ironically, it had been the first one he'd taken in years. He'd gone off to Cheyenne for a few days just to unwind, tied one on at a local saloon one night—something else he rarely did—and picked up this hot little redhead who had killer dimples when she smiled. As the evening progressed, things got a little fuzzy. He was fairly certain, though, that they'd wound up at her place for the night.

The next morning, he made sure he was gone before

she woke up. Less than a week later, he couldn't even remember what the woman's name had been.

And then practically one year to the day, there she was, standing on the doorstep of the mansion wing that was designated for the staff, holding a baby in her arms and saying it was his.

His.

And just like that, he was supposed to take her word for it, supposed to just lie down and accept being someone's parent?

No damn way.

He hadn't even wanted to hold the infant, much less lay claim to it or even find out anything about it. His one-night stand—Joyce, he thought she said her name was—had other ideas, though.

For the most part, Trevor was a man of few words. And even those faded when he was caught off guard— the way he was when Joyce had just shown up out of the blue like that. He was all but speechless—other than saying the word *no,* as in "No, it's not mine." And "No, I won't take her."

After a pointless few minutes of one-sided arguing, Joyce left with the baby. Relieved, he thought that was the end of it. Showed just how naive he was about such things. Because when he walked out again, about twenty minutes later, there was the baby, bundled up and in something Joyce referred to as a "carrier." Joyce herself was nowhere in sight. She'd just left the baby behind and assumed that he would take it from there.

And if that weren't stereotypical enough, there was

a note pinned to the baby's blanket. All that had been missing from the scenario was a snowy scene.

"I've got nobody to help and I can't do this alone," the note had said. "She's yours. You handle it."

That was it. Just sixteen words. Sixteen words that turned his quiet world upside down.

And just like that, he was a father. An *unwilling* father.

"I don't have time for this," he said to the infant now, his deep voice rumbling ominously, like thunder over the plains. "I've got a job to see to and enough responsibilities without you adding to them."

The baby—Avery—responded to his words by howling and crying even harder.

He had no idea how to get her to stop. The least the woman could have done was left some kind of how-to book along with the baby.

He'd done his best to try to locate Joyce again. But there was absolutely no sign of her in the nearby town. He'd gone back to the saloon where he'd initially met her. The bartender there had no clue who she was or where to find her.

Which meant he was stuck with this crying, damp responsibility, one who never seemed to sleep more than five minutes at a time.

"I'm too old for this," he snapped impatiently.

Avery didn't seem to care.

Chapter 1

"You see all this, Cheyenne?" Gabriella Colton said to the three-month-old baby girl she was holding up in her arms.

Gabby moved slowly around in a complete circle, intentionally giving her niece a complete panoramic view of the outdoor area where she was standing. There was nothing but breathtaking scenery as far as the eye could see.

While almost her entire family—as well as most of the staff who worked to keep her father's Wyoming ranch, whimsically christened Dead River Ranch, running smoothly—were presently at the rodeo, Gabby had elected to remain behind and babysit her oldest sister's, Amanda's, daughter.

Staying home hadn't been a hardship for Gabby,

really. She loved children, loved caring for Cheyenne, and she had no great love for rodeos the way the rest of her family did. Attending one would only bring back bad memories that were better left buried. Her first love, Kyle, had thrown her over to join the rodeo circuit as a bronco buster. She had believed him when he'd told her he loved her, discovering that he said the word *love* as frequently as he said "hi." At least he meant the latter, she thought ruefully.

But Gabby didn't want anything bringing her down on this absolutely gorgeous July afternoon, so she'd volunteered to remain at Dead River while everyone else had gone to see wranglers pitting themselves against four-footed competitors.

"Isn't it beautiful, darlin'? This is your grandpa's ranch, and someday, years from now, you'll have a part of it. It's a little quiet now, but that's because everyone's gone to the rodeo. But we don't mind the quiet, do we?" she asked the infant. Cheyenne stared up at her with huge eyes, as if her niece understood every word she said. Gabby liked to think that she did. "When it's quiet like this, we can appreciate how really beautiful this part of the country is."

As Gabby moved from the sprawling courtyard toward the stables, the tranquillity of the afternoon was suddenly shattered with the sound of absolutely heart-wrenching, plaintive wails.

"Uh-oh, looks like I spoke too soon about it being so quiet. Want to go investigate?" she asked the baby. Pretending to receive an affirmative answer, Gabby nodded and said, "That's what I thought. Okay, let's go see what this is all about."

Gabby had taken only a few more steps toward the distressed cries when the source of all that crying became all too apparent.

Trevor Garth, the tall, ruggedly handsome and incredibly silent head of her father's security, came walking out of the small petting zoo, which was being added to the ranch's landscape. As of yet, the zoo was still in the process of being constructed. It was something the ranch hands had begun to put together with the idea that it would be a place for Cheyenne and her little friends to play when she became older.

Trevor's ordinarily somber face sported a pronounced scowl, and it was a toss-up who looked more unhappy, he or the squalling infant in his arms.

When his job didn't force him to interact with someone on the ranch, the dark-haired ex-cop from Cheyenne kept mostly to himself, obviously preferring his own company to that of others. He'd been at Dead River for five years now and had, until just recently, been more or less of a stranger as far as Gabby and the others were concerned.

What had changed in this past month was his status. With one very short but eventful delivery, he'd gone from being a loner to a rather unhappy-looking, unwilling father. One glance at his pained expression right now told Gabby that the man did far better as a loner than a father.

The more the baby in his arms cried, the more at a loss and flustered Trevor seemed to grow.

Gabby had never been able to just look away if she encountered someone in obvious distress. It just wasn't in her to stand around, idle, without trying to remedy the situation. She just wasn't built that way.

"What do you say you and I go rescue Avery's dad?" she asked Cheyenne. The baby gurgled in response and Gabby laughed. "My sentiments exactly. He looks *just* like a fish out of water," she agreed. "But it would be cruel of us just to watch him flounder like that, wouldn't it?" she asked Cheyenne even as she made her way over to the far-from-happy man.

As a man who made it his business to be perpetually aware of his surroundings, Trevor caught the movement out of the corner of his eye and looked in that direction. He was surprised to see his boss's youngest daughter heading his way.

Great, he thought darkly, just what he needed. Little Miss Sunshine to add her voice to the cacophony coming out of his daughter's rosebud mouth.

It wasn't that he actually disliked Gabby Colton. To be honest, he didn't know her well enough to dislike her. Granted, the vibrant redhead was more than a little attractive, but she was also naively optimistic. His opinion was based on the fact that she wholeheartedly wanted to build a center for troubled kids smack-dab in the middle of the ranch, using an empty barn as her starting point.

As if one act of kindness would somehow instantly

transform hardened, cynical street kids into reformed angels.

Ain't gonna happen, he thought sarcastically.

She was still heading toward him. Damn. The last thing he needed was to have the boss's daughter clucking over his so-called daughter, making insipid comments and giving him worse-than-useless advice. He had a feeling that she probably knew even less than he did about child rearing. She seemed like the type that was just interested in spoiling a kid rotten, then later was shocked when that kid turned out to be a self-centered brat.

Oh, hell, what did he know? He supposed that it wasn't quite fair for him to assume something like that. She had to know more than he did.

When she finally reached him, Trevor tipped his black Stetson at her, murmured "Ms. Gabby" politely enough and continued walking.

It took Gabby a moment to summon her courage— there was something really intimidating about the tall, muscular former law-enforcement officer. But his wailing daughter made her forget about her own discomfort, leaving her no choice.

"Trevor, wait," Gabby called out, hurrying to catch up to him. The man had one hell of a lengthy stride, especially when he walked quickly.

It irked Trevor that because he was an employee at the ranch, he had to stop the moment he heard her calling to him. But he was mindful of his position, so he stopped, using up the last of his patience in an effort not to snap out "Yes, ma'am" at the twenty-four-year-old.

"She's really crying up a storm, isn't she?" Gabby said as she caught up to him.

Nothing he found more irritating than someone stating the obvious.

"Certainly sounds that way," Trevor replied, managing to take the edge out of his voice at the last possible moment.

"Do you know why she's crying?" she asked him.

"If I knew why, Ms. Gabby, I'd know how to get her to stop," he answered, measuring out each word carefully and counting the seconds until the young woman left him alone.

"Most likely she's crying because she's cranky and needs a nap."

Avery wasn't the only one. "You think that's it?" he asked out loud. Trevor felt completely wiped out. Being on all-night stakeouts had been far easier than what he'd been going through each night lately. Becoming a father literally overnight and putting up with the exhausting demands of a wailing infant these past two weeks had all but completely drained him to the point that most of the time now, he felt punchy. His last decent night's sleep had occurred *before* she'd been thrust into his arms—literally and figuratively.

"I'm fairly certain," Gabby replied. And then she grinned broadly as an idea hit her. "I tell you what, you hold Cheyenne here and I'll take your daughter and put her down for a nap. Might perk her right up," she predicted. "How's that?" she asked, her grin widening to the point that he thought he was going to fall in.

He inclined his head, ready to agree to anything that would give him even a few minutes' respite. "I'd be in your debt, ma'am."

She rolled her eyes at the salutation he used. "Oh, please. Having you call me 'Ms. Gabby' is bad enough. Please don't call me 'ma'am.' It makes me feel absolutely ancient."

Trevor laughed shortly at the assessment. "Well, if it's one thing you're not, it's ancient," he told her. To him, especially since he had ten years on her, Gabriella Colton was barely older than a child.

Gabby, however, took his response to be on the flirtatious side. Consequently, a slight blush crept up her cheeks. Dusting them with a pink hue.

Clearing her throat, she tried to draw attention away from the momentary infusion of color. "Okay, give me Avery, and you hold Cheyenne for a few minutes."

The shift took a little maneuvering to accomplish since there was nowhere to put either infant down to achieve the swap smoothly.

As he handed over his daughter and took hold of Gabby's tranquil niece, Trevor felt his knuckles brush against something soft.

By the expression on the young woman's face—first startled, then embarrassed—he realized that he'd unwittingly brushed his knuckles against her breasts. That had *not* been his intention.

"Sorry," Trevor mumbled awkwardly.

Gabby murmured a perfunctory "It's okay," deliberately avoiding making any eye contact. She drew his daughter against her, focusing on the infant's wails of distress. "It's okay, sweetheart. We're going to take you inside and make sure you take a nice, peaceful nap. Everything'll be all better when you wake up again. I promise."

The instant his daughter left his arms, Trevor felt relief washing over him. Just to be rid of his wailing burden for even a few minutes felt like a much-longed-for blessing.

Trevor took in a deep breath and let it out slowly. He looked up into Gabby's bright green eyes. "Thanks," he told her dutifully.

Patting the baby's bottom and cooing to her, Gabby glanced over to Avery's father and smiled serenely. "Don't mention it."

She sounded as if she meant it. Obviously crying babies didn't seem to have any effect on her *or* her nerves. That put her one up on him, Trevor couldn't help thinking.

"I'll be right back," Gabby promised, turning on her heel and walking toward the entrance to the main wing of the house. The wing where the Coltons—she, her two older sisters, Amanda and Catherine, and her father— all lived. There was another wing for the staff and wranglers as well as a wing at the very farthest end of the mansion where her father's ex-wife—his third—lived with her two adult children from a previous marriage, Tawny and Trip.

It made for crowded living conditions at times, but

on days like today, when everyone was gone, it felt as if she had an entire castle at her disposal.

Gabby smiled to herself as she entered the house.

Trevor gazed down warily at the infant in his arms. Part of him was waiting for the tiny female to burst into tears. But Cheyenne Colton remained quiet, staring up at him as if he were the newest wonder to come into her world.

"I guess all babies don't cry all the time," Trevor theorized out loud.

Gabby Colton's niece was almost exactly the same age as his newly discovered daughter. But that was where, in his mind, the similarity ended. To his recollection, the infant he was currently holding hardly even whimpered, much less cried.

On the other hand, it seemed as if Avery had done nothing *but* cry in the time she'd been with him. She'd worn away just about all of his nerves—not that he'd had all that many available to begin with.

"Maybe she's just grumpy—like her old man," he guessed out loud.

When he realized that he was actually talking to an infant, he abruptly stopped, feeling somewhat chagrined and annoyed with himself.

Cheyenne looked up at him and gurgled as if to tell him that it was all right.

"You're not really a crybaby, are you?" Gabby said soothingly to the infant she was taking upstairs with her. "It's all just new and scary to you, isn't it? Not that I can actually blame you.

"Your daddy's a really handsome man," Gabby went on. "And he'd look even more so if he just learned to smile once in a while. That scowl of his, though, I've got to admit *is* pretty scary," she said, as if agreeing with something the infant in her arms had just told her. "Don't worry. He'll come around," Gabby promised the baby with certainty. "He'll see what a sweet little thing you can really be once you get used to everything, and his heart can't help but melt then."

Coming to the landing, Gabby made an impulsive decision. "Tell you what, since Cheyenne's already had her nap for the afternoon, why don't we put you in *her* room so you can have a nice roomy crib to sleep in?"

She shifted the infant so that she could look down into the small, round face, as if she were actually gauging the baby's reaction.

"Would you like that, sugar? Sure you would," she told the child. "She's got a room—and a crib—that are really pretty. They're both fit for a little princess. I don't mind telling you that her aunt Catherine and I had a hand in that," Gabby went on proudly, sharing a confidence. "Catherine and I decided that her mommy needed something to cheer her up and get her mind off Cheyenne's daddy taking off before she was even born. He didn't even wait to find out if she was okay," Gabby added sadly. She couldn't understand someone behaving that way and felt that both Amanda and Cheyenne were better off without that man in their lives.

"So we went all out and decorated the nursery as if Cheyenne were really a little princess. Today, *you* get to be that little princess for the afternoon," she told Avery in a purposely breathless voice. The baby's eyes were widening, as if she were literally digesting every word. "How about that, baby girl?" she asked, her smile now spreading from ear to ear.

Gabby's smile grew even wider since the baby had stopped crying and actually seemed to be listening to the sound of her soothing, upbeat cadence.

That was what the baby needed, Gabby decided. To have someone talk to her as if she were a person, not just this—this *thing* to be saddled with, she concluded for lack of a better description.

The only problem was, Gabby thought, how did she go about saying that to Trevor? She knew that the man probably wouldn't take kindly to being told how to act toward his daughter. She doubted if Trevor was the kind to be open to *any* advice at all, constructive or not.

Still, she did have his best interests at heart. His and Avery's. All she wanted to do was just help both of them.

"Maybe he'll feel better after you wake up all rested and happy from your nap. You think so?" she asked. The baby made a noise that sounded a little like a squeak. "No, me neither. But we can always hope for the best, can't we?" she asked.

Leaning against the door, Gabby maneuvered the door lever with her elbow, managing to open it. She then pushed the door open with her back, angling her way into the large, airy bedroom.

The nursery was decorated in all soft pinks and whites. All in all, it did indeed look like a bedroom fit for a princess, right down to the canopied white crib with its delicate musical mobile depicting fairies floating above her.

"Well, here it is, your very own princesslike crib for the afternoon," Gabby declared.

After laying the infant gently down on her back, Gabby began to rub the baby's tummy in slow, concentric circles. It was meant to soothe Avery and help the little girl fall asleep.

Within a few minutes, the soothing, rhythmic motion worked wonders in calming the infant down. Just as she'd hoped.

A couple of whimpers and one near sob later, the little girl's eyes began to flutter shut.

Gabby smiled to herself. "That's my girl—just let it happen. Just let your eyelids get heavy and fall into place. Everything will still be waiting for you when you wake up again. I promise," she added in a soft, melodic whisper.

Several minutes went by. Gabby was fairly sure the baby had fallen asleep.

Just to be certain, Gabby remained standing beside the crib a little longer. She didn't want to take a chance on the infant waking up and wailing again.

Gabby didn't know how anyone else dealt with a crying baby, but she was not partial to the school of thought that chose to ignore the infant for the first few minutes of a crying jag. She instantly picked up Cheyenne any time she heard the baby crying, feeling that it was important to make the infant feel secure and safe. To her way of thinking, picking Cheyenne up when she cried accomplished just that.

So Gabby continued to linger, humming a fragment of a lullaby and massaging Avery's tummy until the sound of the baby's even, steady breathing told her that she really was asleep.

Holding her breath, Gabby quietly tiptoed out of the bedroom, then eased the door closed. She paused for a moment longer, listening at the door.

Satisfied that Avery was indeed fast asleep, Gabby hurried off. She still had a niece to reclaim—not to mention a dour head of security to rescue.

Chapter 2

Trevor wasn't where she'd left him.

Gabby blew out a breath as a sliver of frustration zipped through her.

But then, what did she expect? Dead River's head of security wasn't the type to stand still or be pigeon-holed. And although, even after all this time, she didn't know a great deal about him, she did know that he was unpredictable.

Her fault, Gabby told herself with a sigh. She shouldn't have assumed that since she'd left Trevor standing outside the front of the house, holding her niece, that when she came back, he'd still be there, waiting for her with the baby in his arms.

With her hands on her hips, Gabby impatiently scanned the immediate area in hopes of spotting the man.

She didn't.

The tall, silent ex-cop was apparently nowhere in sight.

"Okay, Mr. Head-of-Security," Gabby said, addressing the air, "if you're not going to be here, waiting for me to come take my niece off your hands, just where *would* you be?"

Gabby glanced over her shoulder at the house she'd just left. It wasn't as if she could just do a quick sweep of it, looking for him. The house where she and her family lived was *huge,* with several wings stretched out across the property. The actual number of rooms within the house had never been pinned down. She could be wandering around for *hours,* especially if Trevor didn't remain stationary himself

Hours? She could literally be playing hide-and-seek with the man for the rest of the month and not stumble across him as long as he was moving around, too.

Gabby chewed her lower lip, frustrated. She should have asked him to stay put, but it had never occurred to her that, since he was holding her niece, he would not just eagerly wait for her to come back so he could be freed of his charge.

No good deed went unpunished, right? Gabby thought sarcastically.

Still looking around the immediate area, Gabby debated what the man's *logical* move would be. She sincerely doubted that he would have taken Cheyenne back to his room in the employees' wing. Somehow, she saw Trevor as wanting his room to remain off-limits to people—*any* people—unless they were specifically invited. Moreover, something told her that she definitely wouldn't make that most likely extremely *short* list.

That left where?

His office! The idea just suddenly occurred to her.

Gabby headed there immediately, mentally crossing her fingers that she was right. Because if Trevor wasn't there, she really didn't have the foggiest where he *might* be and it was getting close to feeding time for Cheyenne. She wanted to find the infant before then.

The little girl had a rather happy disposition, but if she grew hungry, *really* hungry, who knew how she might react? If her niece began fussing the way Avery had, she had a feeling that Trevor would be ready to wipe his hands of any and *all* babies for good—and that certainly wouldn't bode well for Avery's future here at the ranch.

Hurrying back into the house, Gabby made her way through the first floor to the man's small, closetlike office, all the while hoping against hope that she'd find him there with her niece.

As she drew closer to the man's office, Gabby thought she heard the sound of Trevor's voice. It was far too low for her to make out the words, but at least the tone sounded fairly good. The important thing was that he did *not* sound as if he was at the end of his rope, the way he had earlier. And that was definitely good for her niece, and, with any luck, it might also be good for Avery as well.

Gabby approached the cluttered office and saw that

Trevor was sitting at his desk, his chair pushed sufficiently back to accommodate him and the baby he still had in his arms.

From the looks of it, Cheyenne had fallen asleep in his arms.

Gabby stood there for a moment, taking in the scene and wishing she had a camera to preserve the moment. But then, she probably couldn't take the shot anyway. The flash might wake up her niece.

"See, I knew you had it in you," Gabby said out loud to him, although she knew to keep her voice down to a low whisper.

Only maximum control kept Trevor from starting in response to the unexpected sound of her voice.

He'd been too preoccupied, marveling at the peaceful way the infant he was temporarily in charge of had just drifted off to sleep without any encouragement at all. One minute, the baby's incredibly blue eyes were wide open, taking in everything around her, the next minute, they had drifted shut, the long black lashes seemingly resting like soft, silky, spidery crescents on the slight swell of her small, pink cheeks.

A little bit of envy had tugged at his soul when he'd watched her. If he *had* to have a kid, why couldn't he have one like this, he wondered, rather than the wailing banshee he'd got? It was a horrible thing for him to think, but he hadn't asked for this situation.

Nothing ever seemed to take the easy route in his world, Trevor thought in a moment of resigned frustration. Somehow, according to some vast eternal plan, it stood to reason that the cranky kid would be the one he'd wind up with. Maybe this was appropriate.

Lost in thought like that, lamenting his current state and annoyed with himself because of it, Trevor hadn't heard Gabby coming up behind him and, barring the control he could exercise over himself, he would have very nearly jumped.

As it was, it took the man several long seconds to gather himself together sufficiently in order to answer her.

"All I did was hold her," he answered Gabby, turning his swivel chair around so that he faced her. "She did the rest." He nodded at the baby he was holding.

If this Colton woman was trying to flatter him into thinking that he was up to the task of caring for this daughter who had materialized out of nowhere, it wasn't going to work. He knew exactly what he was and wasn't capable of and raising a kid fell into the latter category.

"You're just being modest," Gabby told him, dismissing his words with a careless wave of her hand. She'd never met a man who shied away from taking any credit the way this man did. "I bet you'd be a natural if you just gave yourself half a chance."

Gabby said the words with such conviction, he could only stare at her in absolute wonder. Did she actually believe what she was saying? Or did she just think she could hypnotize him into believing her? Either way, it wasn't happening.

When he finally had a chance to get a word in edgewise, all he could do was shake his head. And then, curious, he had to ask, "Do your horses ever come back to the stable?"

Because he'd worked the streets as a police officer, he'd come across a lot of people in his time, but he could honestly say that he had never met anyone who just radiated supreme optimism and babbled incessantly about everything eventually being right in the world. Gabriella Colton did just this. Every bit of her seemed hell-bent on brightening her surroundings. For his part, he'd seen too much of life's underbelly to dip into that well water the boss's youngest daughter was drinking. People were either good or bad, and given a choice between the two, people usually went with the latter.

He also believed that if anything could go wrong, it did. What that meant in this case was that most likely, Avery's mother was *not* going to come back for her. Which, in turn, meant that he was going to be stuck with a baby unless he could figure a way out of this situation.

Right now, he was thinking about giving her up for adoption. She stood a better chance with parents who wanted her and were willing to learn what it took to take care of her. He didn't have the time or the patience—or the financial fortune—to raise a kid.

It took Gabby a couple of moments to figure out what the man was saying to her.

Rather than take offense at his tone, she smiled and said, "Yes, actually my 'horses' *do* come back to the stable," she said, using his metaphor. "But then," she continued, deliberately smiling as widely as she could, "I just take them out for another ride."

He shook his head. "It figures," he snorted. The woman was clearly flighty. What did she know about life—or hardship? But then, he supposed there was something almost admirable about her rabid determination to remain so upbeat in the face of everything—including the self-centered, wounded-bear of a father she had. Living in the Colton family was no easy feat.

"You put the kid to bed in my room?" he asked.

Faye Frick, the Colton's head nanny for the past couple of decades, had unearthed an extra crib for Avery and had it brought to his room.

Faye had a way of looking out for all of them, he recalled fondly, though his expression never changed. He cared about Faye a great deal.

Years ago, the widow had taken it upon herself to raise him when his own father, a former wrangler at Dead River, had dumped him and taken off for parts unknown. He'd been all of fourteen at the time and determined to live on his own, although the state had other ideas about the way he would spend his next four years. He would have been swallowed up by the system if it hadn't been for Faye.

Consequently, he had always had a soft spot in his heart for the older woman, but it still didn't mellow his rather abrupt way of interacting with all the other people around him.

"Actually, no, I didn't put her in your room," Gabby replied.

His dark brows narrowed as his eyes bored into her. "Where *did* you put her to bed?" he asked, even as he told himself it really didn't matter where the kid was sleeping, as long as she wasn't here, hollering in his ear.

Gabby couldn't help looking rather pleased with herself for having thought of this. "I thought I'd treat your daughter to a nap in Cheyenne's crib—in her nursery," she specified, just in case Trevor didn't make the connection right away.

The man might be head of security, but she suspected that incidental details like cribs with canopies and specially decked-out nurseries were completely under his radar.

"You didn't think the one she has was good enough?" he asked.

Trevor's sharply worded question caught her completely by surprise. He was unnerving her again, she realized, and she'd almost stepped back, away from the scowl she saw looming over his brow.

She had to stop that. Stop avoiding confrontation. She was a Colton and she would be running that center for troubled teens soon enough. They weren't all going to tiptoe around her just because she was trying to do something decent and charitable for them. They would come on angry and resentful at times—just as this man was doing right now.

If she didn't learn how to stand up to him and stand up for herself, then she might as well pack it in right now, Gabby reasoned. She had to learn not to come across as a spineless wimp.

Her voice quavered at first, but it took on strength as she continued to speak. "I meant no disrespect, Trevor. But Cheyenne's nursery looks like something a princess would sleep in, and I thought it would be an uplifting change of scenery for Avery to take her nap in that room."

"And you really think she's supposed to notice the difference?" he asked incredulously. "At three months?" Trevor pressed, emphasizing the ludicrousness of her thought process.

Gabby refused to back down. "Maybe," she countered, adding, "Subconsciously."

"Yeah, right," he all but jeered.

And then Trevor stopped abruptly, taking stock of what he was saying. He supposed, in her own way, the Colton woman meant no harm and probably thought she was doing a good deed. From what he knew of her—and had heard—it wasn't in the youngest of the Colton women to thumb her nose at the difference in their stations in life.

Handing over her niece, he murmured, "I didn't mean to go off on you like that. I grew up not having much. There were those who liked to rub my nose in it. I guess that made me kind of thin-skinned when it comes to certain things."

Her heart instantly ached for the boy he had once been.

"Well, I was *not* trying to rub your nose in anything,"

she told him in a voice that all but throbbed with compassion, even as Gabby stated her case assertively.

"Yeah, I know," he told her in a low voice that was utterly devoid of any indications of emotion. "And if the kid *could* notice her surroundings, she'd probably not want to come back to the room she has," he acknowledged. "Most likely it definitely isn't anywhere *near* as fancy as your niece's."

"Don't be so hard on yourself," Gabby said in a firm voice he couldn't remember ever hearing come out of her mouth. "There are a lot more important things in life than pretty bedrooms and fancy cribs. They certainly don't make up for the lack of a parent's love," she maintained.

Gabby was admittedly thinking of her own situation. Her mother had just taken off one day, abandoning her and her sisters without so much as a backward glance while her father, whom she stubbornly loved even though at times the man definitely did *not* deserve it, had a very hard time showing any of them so much as a thin sliver of affection.

And while she, Catherine and Amanda didn't lack for anything material, emotional connection with a parent was a whole different story. There were times when she felt almost *starved* for a display, no matter how small, of parental approval. It was, she felt, what a lot of kids strove for—and what they grew up missing. It was what made her so eager to help underprivileged kids.

Belatedly, Gabby read between the lines. "Does this mean you've made up your mind to keep her?" she wondered out loud, asking the question with a degree of excitement that unsettled him.

There she went, off on another tangent, he thought in barely restrained annoyance. Why couldn't the woman just take things at face value instead of making mountains out of molehills?

"It doesn't mean anything at all," he told her in a flat, distant voice. "I was trying to be polite and apologize. Don't look for any hidden meanings in that—because there aren't any. Why are you grinning?" he asked. Was she laughing at him?

Her grin only grew wider, as if she were harboring a secret and he didn't have the first clue what it was. "You come on all mean and tough," she told him, "but deep down inside, there's this other layer—"

"—that's just as mean and just as tough," he concluded with finality. Placing a wide palm on each armrest, he pushed himself out of his chair and to his feet. "Now, if you'll excuse me, I've got rounds to make. With the ranch this empty, it would be a perfect time for some yahoos to come barging in and try to steal something or do something they shouldn't."

Holding the sleeping infant to her cheast, Gabby put a protective hand around Cheyenne and looked at him, a little of her smile fading. Up until now, she'd felt incredibly safe here at home. Now he was giving her cause if not for alarm, then at least for concern.

"You really think there's something to worry about?" she asked.

He shrugged, his wide shoulders rising and falling in

an asymmetrical movement. "Better safe than sorry, I always say. The guy next door isn't looking to 'love his neighbor.' He's looking to take advantage of his neighbor, maybe steal from him if that neighbor happens to be rich—like you and your family," he added pointedly.

The expression on his face left no room for argument.

She did anyway. It had never been in her nature to accept pessimism at face value. "That's a horrible way to look at life," she protested.

"Horrible?" He pretended to consider the word, then dismissed it with a "Maybe." Trevor said the word for her sake. He didn't consider it horrible at all. To him, it was just the way life was. "But realistic?" he continued. "You bet. The sooner you wrap your head around that, Miss Colton, the sooner you'll be able to come face-to-face with reality."

Gabby raised her chin. "I don't like your reality, Mr. Garth."

He surprised her by saying, "Me neither. But that doesn't change the facts as I see them," he told her.

"If that's what you think, then it's no wonder you're always scowling," she told him.

"Wasn't aware that I was," he lied. "Now, you got anything else you want to tell me, or can I go on my rounds?"

"Only that it wouldn't hurt you to try to change your attitude a little, look on the bright side once in a while."

"I will when they get a little brighter," he answered, picking up his Stetson from his desk.

"They?" she questioned.

"The bad guys," he clarified, then added, "The ones I'm providing your family security against. Your rosy world would be real to me if these guys went away." He brought the irony full circle.

Gabby sighed and tried one more time, feeling as if there were more at stake here than just winning a philosophical argument. She had the distinct impression that the state of his soul was in play here.

Trevor just couldn't be satisfied being this disgruntled, this dark in his outlook, in his take on life, she thought. Could he?

There had to be a way to get through to him, to get him to come around, even if only a little, to her mindset. There just *had* to be.

To that end, Gabby began racking her brain to find it.

"Maybe there aren't as many bad guys as you think," she told him, adding that she needed just a little more time to get this right and convince him, bring him around to her way of thinking—or at the very least, a little closer to her way of thinking.

"And maybe there are a lot more of them than *you* think," he countered. His eyes seemed to pin her in place for a moment, leaving her nowhere to turn away. "Did you ever consider that?"

Rather than cave, she answered firmly, "No," as she tossed her head for emphasis.

"Didn't think so," he muttered under his breath as he tipped the brim of his hat to her. With that, he left the room.

"There goes one unhappy man, Cheyenne," she murmured softly to the baby in her arms.

Cheyenne just continued sleeping. The baby didn't know how lucky she was.

Chapter 3

He supposed, in an odd sort of way, he had to admire the youngest Colton woman, Trevor thought approximately an hour later as he started to head back to his office once again.

Dumb though the subject of her focus seemed to him, Gabriella Colton *did* appear to know what she wanted, what she believed in.

And, more impressively, she'd actually stood up to him rather than cave in the face of his disapproving judgment of those beliefs she held so dear.

Not all that many people actually stood up to him when push came down to shove. He had a way of making people back off without his having to resort to physical action. Just his attitude—coupled with a dark, contemptuous scowl—usually did the trick.

Despite her soft, attractive appearance, Gabby Colton was one hell of a feisty female; he'd have to give her that.

Now, as far as being smart, well, that was a whole different story, Trevor mused as he made his way back across the grounds.

How the hell she could believe in goodness and light when she was surrounded by all sorts of wheelers and dealers, not to mention people like her old man, a black-hearted, womanizing devil if ever he'd come across one, was just beyond him.

Granted, there were good people here on the ranch, like Faye, who'd raised him when there was nothing in it for her beyond being guilty of a good deed, and like her sister Amanda, the baby's mother, whose only sin was letting herself be sweet-talked by the wrong guy.

But then there were people around like her father's third ex-wife, Darla, and Darla's two adult kids from some previous marriage, Tawny and Trip. All three were worthless parasites, one worse than the other, in his opinion.

He still couldn't figure out why the old man allowed those three to stay on. Ordinarily, he would have expected Jethro to send all three of them packing the second the ink had dried on the divorce papers—ending a marriage that had barely managed to pass the one-year anniversary. Instead, the old man had set the trio up to live in one of the extended wings.

Trevor laughed shortly. That kind of thing clearly smelled of blackmail to him. Which meant one of the three—most likely Darla—had something to hold over the boss's head—which in turn meant that the old man had done something pretty damn bad.

Not that that surprised him.

The lot of them, Darla, Tawny and Trip, weren't worth even a plugged nickel. They just didn't fit in with the rest of them. All three of them looked as if they'd been transplanted from some bad, made-in-one-afternoon movie about grifters. They reminded him of vultures, circling carrion and just waiting for it to die so they could swoop down and tear off its flesh. He didn't trust any of them any farther than he could throw them. Less. And yet there was starry-eyed Gabby, not just *talking* about starting up a center for troubled teens but actually *working* toward that goal and trying to convince the old man to have the center built right here, converting an old barn he had on his property.

That kind of drive either took an absolute fool—which he didn't think Gabby was—or it took someone who saw only the good in people.

He figured it had to be the latter.

That made her too good to deal with the likes of the majority of the people living on or around the Dead River Ranch.

Frowning, Trevor shrugged away the thought. This was way too complicated for him to sort through, and it was pointless to waste his time that way. It was what it was, and besides, he had his own dilemma to untangle and come to grips with, namely what to do with the kid he was suddenly saddled with.

If he experienced any parental stirrings toward her—she *was* rather cute when she wasn't crying—he banked them down. He—and more importantly, she—couldn't afford to have them. It just wasn't in the little girl's best interest to remain here, so there was no sense in allowing himself to feel anything at all for her.

There was no doubt in his mind that he would make a really poor father, and a kid needed a father—and a mother, too, something else he couldn't give Avery. As far as he saw, the only logical conclusion to be reached was that Avery needed to be adopted and raised by someone other than him—preferably *two* "someones."

In the interim, maybe he should get over his pride, stop trying to handle this on his own and ask Faye for help, Trevor thought. She'd always been the sensible one, stable even when everything else looked as if it was just going to hell in the proverbial hand basket. She'd stepped right in not just in his case, but also when the Colton girls' mother, Mandy, decided to take off, leaving the ranch—and them—ten years ago. It was Faye who made sure they didn't lack for attention, didn't feel abandoned. Faye would know what he needed to do to ensure that Avery was not just looked after, but well taken care of, too.

After all, he didn't just want to dump the kid. None of this was her fault. She hadn't asked to be born, right? Trevor reflected silently. Just like *he* hadn't asked to become a father.

Life had a way of making things happen, but he didn't have to just stand there and take it. There had to be options, decent options, he reasoned, in order to make things right.

He and Faye would find Avery a good home and that would be the end of it.

With his game plan roughly in place, Trevor went into his office. There was some paperwork he still needed to catch up on. It was his least favorite thing to do, but he decided that he might as well utilize the peace and quiet he found himself in while it lasted. He'd be listening to Avery howl soon enough.

Trevor glanced at his watch and realized that at this point he'd had over two hours of sweet silence and freedom from the daunting burden of fatherhood. He wasn't exactly eager to get caught up in it again, but on the other hand, he'd never been one to shirk his responsibilities, no matter how oppressive or annoying they might be.

Maybe he'd be lucky and Avery would still be sleeping, although he sincerely doubted it. In the short time he'd had the infant, he couldn't remember a single instance when Avery had slept more than ninety minutes at a clip, much less over two hours. To expect that it could go on indefinitely was just plain wishful thinking on his part and completely unrealistic.

Trevor sighed as he pushed himself away from his desk and squared his shoulders. Time to face the music.

Literally.

Since Gabby was so good with kids and didn't seem to mind being around them, maybe he'd see if he could get her to volunteer her services again—soon. Oh, he wouldn't come out and actually *ask* her to mind Avery for him, but if he happened to show up somewhere in her vicinity and Avery was howling like last time, he had a pretty good hunch that Gabby would take it upon herself to put the kid—and him—out of their misery and just take over. She wasn't the type to leave well enough alone or ignore a situation that needed remedying. He figured she had what they called a type A personality and just couldn't help herself when it came to taking over.

Trevor smiled to himself as he left his office and went toward the main wing of the house.

Who knew, maybe some kind of a satisfactory arrangement could even be reached between him, Gabby and Faye regarding Avery. Then he wouldn't have to give her up for adoption.

Have to?

The phrase he'd just used came echoing back to him in his head.

Since when did he *have to* give the kid up for adoption? He *wanted* to give her up for adoption, he reminded himself.

At least, that was what he *thought* he wanted.

Damn it, the situation he was facing was getting him all jumbled up inside, he thought, annoyed with himself as well as the situation. He'd been spun around so many times, he didn't know which way was up, which way was down anymore.

That had to change.

The kid was going up for adoption and that was that, he concluded. He couldn't be a dad—who did he think he was kidding to even *consider* that? He *never* undertook anything unless he thought he had a chance of getting it right. There was no chance like that in this case. He had no example to follow, no fond memories to tap into. He certainly wasn't about to emulate the father who'd dumped him on the Colton doorstep.

Annoyed, Trevor blew out a breath as he came closer to the nursery. This whole thing was getting damn confusing and really *way* out of hand. He had to stop overthinking it. He was going to put Avery up for adoption and that was that.

As Trevor drew closer to the closed door, nothing but a wall of silence greeted him. The corners of his mouth curved slightly.

He assumed the kid was still asleep after all.

That had to be a good sign. Maybe keeping her around wouldn't be all that ba—

His thoughts were abruptly shut down as a scream suddenly tore through the silence.

The scream, followed by another, louder one, was coming from the nursery.

Instantly, Trevor broke into a run before the full import of the scream and what it could mean had a chance to sink in.

The door was unlocked and he yanked it open. The first thing he saw was Gabby on her knees in the middle of the nursery.

Obviously struggling to regain control over herself, Gabby was staring at the body she was kneeling over. Blood pooled around the body's upper torso and it was steadily leaching into Gabby's jeans where she was kneeling.

She didn't seem to realize it.

Drawing closer, Trevor looked at the victim's face. His lunch swiftly rose in his throat, threatening to come out, and he felt as if someone had stuck a hot poker into his gut and was twisting it.

The body on the floor was Faye. The short black hair she always kept so neatly was in complete disarray, a casualty of the physical struggle that had obviously taken place. Small-boned and slender, it was apparent that she had still fought like a tiger.

And lost.

There was no pulse when he felt for it in the woman's neck. The expression on her lifeless face was a combination of anger and horror.

The exact same emotions he was now feeling, multiplied by ten.

Trevor realized that Gabby was desperately trying to stop the flow of blood from the woman's chest with her hands. Both were covered with Faye's blood. It was a futile undertaking.

"She's dead," he told her, his tone harsher than it should have been in order to mask his own pain.

"No, she's not," Gabby insisted frantically through her tears. "She's alive." Her tears fell, mingling with the dead woman's blood. "We can keep her alive! Maybe if we—"

Trevor didn't let her finish. Instead, grasping the back of her collar, he physically pulled Gabby away from the lifeless body.

"She's dead," he repeated a bit more gently this time, stepping back from his own grief and seeing the pain and tears that were in Gabby's eyes. "There's nothing you can do for her now," he told her, drawing Gabby up to her feet.

Gabby's knees suddenly buckled, giving way. Reacting, Trevor caught her and pulled her against him without thinking. For an instant, Gabby broke down, sobbing and clutching on to him for support.

"Who could have done this to her?" she asked between sobs. "Why would anyone want to hurt Faye? She was always so good to everyone."

"I don't know," he answered, seething. There was now an entire myriad of emotions rushing and flashing through him like so many fireworks on a collision course.

As he stroked Gabby's hair in an awkward attempt to comfort the sobbing woman, he looked around the rest of the room.

And suddenly froze.

This isn't right.

"Where's the kid?" he asked Gabby sharply.

Pulling herself together, Gabby drew her head back, blinked several times to clear her vision and then turned in the direction of the crib.

Her brain muddled by grief and confusion, she wasn't sure she'd heard his question correctly.

"What?" she asked thickly.

"The kid. *My* kid," Trevor bit off with harsh emphasis. Dropping his arms from around Gabby as if he hadn't just paused to give her comfort, he strode quickly over to the fancy, canopied crib. "Where's my kid?" he demanded hotly.

The crib was empty.

Trevor swung around to glare at Gabby, waiting for her to offer some sort of an answer.

"I thought you said that you put Avery down in this crib." It came out sounding like an accusation, not a question.

"I did," she cried.

Everything inside of her was shaking. Seeing Faye on the floor, bloodied and motionless, had blocked out everything else. She hadn't even realized that the crib was empty or that the baby was missing.

Oh, God, how could she have missed that?

"I just came in to check on her when I saw Faye—when I saw Faye—"

Gabby couldn't bring herself to finish the sentence. A sob threatened to break free in her throat and it took everything she had to get herself under control and push it back down.

Like a man trapped in a nightmare not of his own making, Trevor moved back to the crib again. This time he realized that although there was no baby in it, the crib wasn't completely empty. One of the knitting needles he recognized as belonging to Faye was stabbed into an embroidered pillow.

The knitting needle was anchoring down a note.

His first impulse was to rip the note away from the pillow, but he forced himself to refrain. He knew that the chief of police would need the note untouched, the better to dust the surface for any fingerprints, partial or otherwise. The slightest piece of evidence could eventually lead them to Faye's killer.

And he wanted to slowly fillet whoever that turned out to be.

Very carefully, making sure not to touch anything and consequently add to the fingerprints he knew had to already be on the paper, Trevor leaned in over the crib and read what was written in block letters on the note: WAIT FOR RANSOM INSTRUCTIONS. ONE MISSTEP, THE KID'S DEAD.

It wasn't until he stepped back that he realized Gabby was right behind him. He wound up backing right into her. The imprint of her body against his back registered without warning.

Swallowing a curse, he turned to glare at her. "Be careful," he snapped. "I could have knocked you down or at the very least, crushed your foot."

Gabby waved away his words. Neither occurrence would have been of any consequence to her. She'd just read the note left in the crib and her heart had all but turned to lead at the implication.

It made no sense to her. But then, evil never really did.

"Why would they want to kidnap your daughter?" she asked, bewildered.

"They wouldn't," he bit off, his tone emotionless. "They think they've got *your* niece."

The shock his words created almost undid her. Gabby covered her mouth to keep back another distressed cry. Her eyes widened with horror. "Oh, my God. They made a mistake."

"Yeah," he agreed grimly.

And the consequences of that mistake echoed through his head, loud and clear. The moment the kidnappers realized that they'd made that mistake, Avery became worthless to them.

Trevor refused to follow that train of thought to the end. It was far too awful to contemplate, even for a fleeting second.

He needed to get Avery back.

Suddenly, the child he hadn't wanted less than an hour ago became very precious to him.

Beside him, Gabby was struggling not to break down again. Hysteria wouldn't help get Avery back. She drew in a long breath and then let it out slowly, repeating the process one more time.

Somewhat more in control, she turned to Trevor. When she thought about it, she could see why the mistake had been made. "They're the same age, the same coloring—"

Was she making a case for the kidnapper's mistake, or was she trying to convince him that the mistake wouldn't come to light and then his daughter would stay safe indefinitely?

"But not the same kid," he all but ground out, pointing out the obvious.

Not the same kid.

And that was her fault. While she was grateful that Cheyenne was safely lying in the crib she had put into her own bedroom, Gabby felt beyond guilty that Trevor's daughter had been mistakenly kidnapped in Cheyenne's place.

"What are we going to do?" she asked him breathlessly.

We.

As if they were in this thing together, Trevor thought with contempt. But they weren't in this together. That was *his* daughter who had been kidnapped and the woman who had raised *him* who had been killed. It was in no way the same thing.

Yes, Faye had taken care of Gabby and her sisters, but she'd been paid to do that. No one had paid her to take care of him. She'd done that out of the goodness of her heart, without expecting any sort of compensation from anyone—and getting none.

He couldn't even remember the last time he'd thanked Faye for anything—her, the woman to whom he'd owed so much.

Anger—at the world and at himself—all but choked off his windpipe.

It took Trevor a few moments to get himself under control again. When he did, he pulled his cell phone out of his rear pocket.

"*We're* going to call the police chief," he told her,

deliberately emphasizing the word *we* in a mocking tone—bravado and anger were all he had left right now, "and tell him what happened. He can take it from there once he gets here."

Gabby didn't know which way to turn, what to do with herself.

She didn't want to just do *nothing,* didn't want to just stand back and let someone else take over. This was *her* fault. She was the one who had *left* Avery in this room. It was all on *her.* There had to be something— some small contribution to the whole—that she could be doing right now.

To do absolutely nothing felt as if she were just compounding her sin, making her feel more guilty for what had happened.

She couldn't handle it.

Gabby looked at him, her expression bordering on frantic. "Isn't there anything we—?"

"No!" he snapped before she could finish. "There isn't anything we can do right now except what I'm doing." He punched the chief's number on his keyboard.

Nodding, numbed and at a loss, Gabby fell silent and backed off.

Chapter 4

Police chief Hank Drucker made the fifteen-mile trip from the town of Dead—located approximately forty miles northwest of Cheyenne—to the ranch in record time.

He had moved quickly because the call had come from the Colton ranch—no one ever ignored the Coltons—and because there'd been a kidnapping. An infant was currently missing.

Drucker liked kids, even though he and his wife, Harriet, had never had any of their own. Whatever other failings and flaws he might have had, Drucker believed that children—especially babies—should be protected at all cost.

The chief, a big man whose out-of-shape body was a clear testimonial that his prime had long since past, looked as if he were born on the job. After thirty-two years on the Dead Police Department—working his way from the ground up, he might as well have been. Being a policeman was all he'd ever known, all he'd ever been. The life suited him.

This was going to be messy, he thought as he came in. He knew he was going to have to tread very cautiously— for reasons that wouldn't be apparent to anyone else but him and one other person.

Walking into the nursery, Drucker didn't stop to confer with either Trevor or Gabby. Instead, he went directly to Faye's body. The chief crouched down as best he could, given that his knees were acting up and his expanding girth showed them no mercy.

"Damn shame," he muttered under his breath, shaking his head. He'd known the fifty-year-old governess for over two decades.

With a barely suppressed groan, he got back up to his feet. "Looks like she must've surprised whoever it was in the act and tried to stop them from making off with the baby—and got killed for her trouble," he concluded grimly. "My guess is that we're dealing with one or more hotheaded kidnappers—always a bad combination."

Turning away for a second, the chief barked out a few orders to the two officers he'd brought with him, Karen Locke and Pierce DeLuca, and they began to secure the crime scene—as they had come to understand the term. Neither one looked as if he or she were capable of an independent thought.

Drucker, meanwhile, decided that now was the time to ask a few preliminary questions. "You hear anything?" he asked Trevor.

Trevor shook his head, silently cursing himself for allowing this to have happened on his watch. Aside from the victim being his daughter, this was his territory. He was responsible for everything that came or went at Dead River. Responsible for everything *on* it as well. There were no excuses for dropping the ball the way that he had.

"I was in my office before I came up here. Before that, I took a turn around the property. And no, I didn't see anything out of the ordinary," Trevor answered, anticipating the chief's next question.

Drucker laughed shortly, although there was no humor in the sound. "I keep forgetting you were a big-city cop once upon a time." There was a trace of mocking in the chief's voice. His tone was definitely *not* warm and friendly. "Place seems pretty empty," he noted. "Where is everybody? At the rodeo?" he asked and answered his own question.

"Yes," Gabby answered in a shaky voice. "I thought Faye was supposed to be there, too." At least, that was what the woman had told her. Her son, Dylan, was working with some of the animals at the rodeo, and predominantly, she had gone to see him in action. It was no secret that Faye was very proud of her son.

Gabby was still struggling to come to grips with what had happened. Finding Faye the way she had and the staggering weight of her guilt at accidentally having placed Avery in harm's way were almost too much for her to bear.

In the fifteen minutes that they had waited for Drucker to arrive, she had dashed to her room to reassure herself that Cheyenne was still there and still all right. Unwilling to leave the infant alone for a moment after all this had happened, she'd picked up her niece and brought her back to the scene of Avery's abduction. She took painstaking care to keep Cheyenne from even so much as glancing in the direction of the gruesomely murdered governess.

"Heard the rodeo was pretty good this year. Why didn't you go, Ms. Colton?" Drucker asked mildly, as if he were just shooting the breeze with her.

Gabby knew the chief well enough to know that he was not as entirely laid-back as he attempted to appear. He was taking in and measuring her every word. It made her feel like a suspect.

The absurdity of that was beyond any words she had at her disposal.

"I don't much like rodeos," she told the chief as calmly as possible.

Drucker met her comment with a careless shrug, then glanced over toward Trevor. "Guess they're not for everyone. How about you, Garth?" he asked abruptly, craning his neck to look at the ranch's head of security. "Why didn't you go to the rodeo? Or don't you like them, either?"

They were making small talk—he didn't care how much Drucker thought he could use this useless line of questioning to lead them to the truth; it wasn't anywhere near fast enough.

"Don't think much about them one way or another," he said, answering the chief's previous question. "I was here—at the ranch—because I had a brand-new kid on my hands and I had to take care of her."

Drucker listened quietly, and when Trevor paused, the chief asked rhetorically, "And she was the one who was kidnapped, right?"

"Right," Trevor ground out between clenched teeth. It was hard suppressing the desire to say a few choice words to the smaller man. He didn't need the chief rubbing his nose in the fact that his daughter had been abducted under his watch.

"Doesn't seem like you had much luck taking care of her, does it?" The rhetorical question had the corners of Drucker's mouth curving. "Anybody have it in for you, Garth? Some employee you fired or an unhappy maid you might have paid a little too much or too little attention to?" Drucker pressed.

Gabby spoke up, interrupting the chief's questions. "The kidnappers didn't know they were taking his daughter."

Interest heightened in the chief's dark-circled eyes. "Oh? And why's that?"

This was the hard part. It took everything she had not to just break down, or melt down, or whatever the current correct term for this sick feeling she presently had going on in the pit of her stomach.

"Because I put Avery down for a nap in Cheyenne's crib."

Drucker turned to look at her, a spark of fresh interest in the man's tired eyes. "And why would you do something like that?" he asked.

Another wave of frustration and helplessness washed over Gabby. If only she hadn't done this, if only she'd put the baby in the crib Faye had found for her, Avery would still be safe, and Faye wouldn't have had to sacrifice her life trying to save the infant.

If only...

She was making herself crazy. *Just answer the question,* Gabby silently ordered.

"I thought I was doing something nice for her. I would have never dreamed I was putting her in any sort of danger. If I'd had the slightest inkling, then I wouldn't have—"

"Of course you wouldn't," the chief acknowledged kindly, politely cutting her off. "Nobody ever expects these kinds of things to happen to them. Just like those kidnappers didn't expect to take the wrong baby," he emphasized. "Hell of a surprise for them when they realize they did."

The panic Gabby was trying so hard to bank down began to flare up again, threatening to consume her.

"Do you think they will realize it?" With each word she uttered, she talked faster, as if she were trying to outrun the idea, the suggestion that the kidnappers would suddenly be struck by the difference in the two infants, which was minimal at best. "The babies do look alike and they're the same age—maybe the kidnappers won't even notice."

There was an expression of pity on Drucker's face, as if he couldn't see how she could believe the charade would continue indefinitely. There was a very real fly in the ointment. "They'll notice when your daddy refuses to pay the ransom, saying his grandbaby is all nice and snug at Dead River."

The horror of the scenario he'd just tossed out so cavalierly appalled Gabby.

"My father won't refuse to pay to get Avery back," she insisted. The idea was too terrible for her to entertain even for a moment.

The look of pity briefly intensified in the chief's gray eyes. "We talking about the same Jethro Colton?" he asked with a barely suppressed smirk. "'Cause the one I know would have trouble parting with money to rescue his own kin. There's no way he'd do it to bring back someone else's," Drucker stated flatly.

Gabby raised her chin, something within her temporarily galvanizing. She refused to accept what Drucker was saying. That would make her father a monster. "You're wrong."

The chief shook his head, as if he thought she was being delusional, but for now he kept that to himself. Instead, he looked at Trevor.

"For your daughter's sake, I sure hope so." But his very tone said that he sincerely doubted that he *was* wrong.

It was at that moment, while the chief was predicting

Jethro Colton's far-from-stellar reaction to the situation, that Trevor suddenly realized the truth of his feelings.

He wasn't resentful of the burden Avery represented or indifferent to her existence. The thought of possibly permanently losing Avery made him come to grips with the fact that he actually *loved* the little girl. What he'd been struggling with these past two weeks was not that he didn't want her but that he realized this tiny little human being was going to wind up changing the whole world as he knew it.

But now, if the chief's prediction *was* right, Avery might never get that chance to change his whole world. Never get the chance to grow up, to experience her first kiss, her first love. Never be any of the things that she was meant to be.

Not unless *he* found a way to rescue her.

"You're wrong," Gabby repeated with feeling, catching Trevor's eye. "My father won't withhold the ransom money."

Right then, they heard the sound of cars—a large number of cars—approaching the house.

The chief went to the window and looked out. "Looks like we're about to find out which one of us is right about your daddy, little lady," he said to Gabby. "You two keep on taking pictures of anything that looks out of order—and *don't touch the body,*" he emphasized, instructing the two officers to continue with their work. "That's for the medical examiner to do."

With that, he left the room, moving at a slightly

faster pace than he normally assumed. Watching the man brought the term *slow but steady* to mind.

Drucker got down to the bottom of the stairs just as the front door opened and the various members of the Colton family, as well as their staff, began to fill up the vast foyer.

Seeing the police chief among them created confusion, and a cacophony of voices mingled together, each asking questions.

It was Mathilda Perkins, the head housekeeper, who had been the first to notice Drucker. Mathilda had been running the main house as well as the staff for as long as anyone could remember, and her sharp eyes took possession of any room she entered.

She missed nothing.

"What are you doing here, Chief?" she asked, suspicion entering her voice. "Thought you might have been at the rodeo. Riders were in top form—" She stopped abruptly at the sight of the chief's grim expression. "Is something wrong?" The last vestiges of cheerfulness had left her voice, and she sounded far more somber— and somewhat apprehensive as she waited for a response to her question.

"'Fraid so," the chief began.

Jethro Colton pushed his way to the front of the crowd. "Well, out with it, man," he ordered gruffly. "Don't play out the suspense, trying to make yourself look like some sort of metropolitan supersleuth. You're a small-town, plodding tin star. Now, what the hell is going on?" he demanded coldly. "Some of us are tired and not interested in cheap drama."

It was Trevor, rather than the chief, who answered Jethro's insensitive question. During his law-enforcement career, both in Cheyenne and on the ranch, he had never learned how to deftly soften a blow or say something other than just shooting straight from the hip. He followed his instincts now.

"It's Faye, Mr. Colton."

Jethro's eyes squinted, all but boring into his security head's very countenance. "Faye? What about her?" He looked around. "Where is she, anyway? I told her she could ride in my car to and from the rodeo, but right in the middle, she starts to worry about 'her babies,'" he jeered, the term referring to both his granddaughter and to Trevor's daughter. "Next thing I know, she's taking off. So she did come back," he concluded, appearing somewhat disgruntled. He wasn't a man who took being disregarded lightly.

"Yes, sir, she did come back," Trevor replied, so much emotion warring within him that he sounded all but paralyzed inside a monotone prison as he answered, "She's been murdered."

"She's been what?" Jethro shouted angrily, as if someone on his staff had acted independently, indifferent to his edicts. His voice grew in volume as he demanded, "What the hell are you talking about?"

At the same time Mathilda shrieked, "Oh, my God, no!" Her knees apparently buckled and she fell to the floor, sobbing and rocking to and fro.

Cries of horror and disbelief echoed throughout the foyer as the rest of the people who had just come in tried to assimilate the information that one of their own had been killed.

A flood of questions all but bounced off the very walls as well as the people within them.

"Who did it?"

"Why would anyone kill Faye?"

"Are you sure?"

"Dead? Really dead?"

"Oh, God. Are we all in danger?"

Others, severely numbed by the news, said nothing, only listened, waiting either to be convinced or given details. Or, better yet, for someone to tell them they were dreaming.

No one could believe that she was really dead. They had just seen her early this morning, talking and as full of life as ever.

"Why would someone kill her?" Catherine, one of Gabby's two older sisters, asked, her voice shaky as she asked the question.

"Apparently she was in the wrong place at the wrong time," the chief said, speaking up. His authoritative tone indicated that he had the floor now. "Looks like she tried to stop the kidnapping."

"What kidnapping?" someone from the staff cried.

"There's been a kidnapping?" Jethro's question sounded more like an accusation that the chief had been withholding information from him.

Amanda all but went into shock. She covered her

mouth with her hands to hold back the guttural cry that was clawing at her throat, seeking release.

"Oh, my God, my baby," she cried, her eyes darting toward Gabby. She'd gone to the rodeo only because she trusted Gabby implicitly and Gabby was supposed to be babysitting.

But then she realized that her sister was holding a baby. That was *her* baby. Then what was the chief talking about?

Rushing over to take her baby from Gabby, Amanda scooped the infant into her arms, holding on to her as tightly as she dared. The sudden, terrified ache in her heart abated.

"No," the chief said. "As you can see, your little lady wasn't the victim. She stayed nice and safe and sound." For emphasis he needlessly gestured toward Gabby just as Amanda took hold of her little girl.

It took Amanda more than a few seconds to reconcile the alternative waves of terror and exhilaration going through her, neutralizing the effects. All that mattered, she told herself, taking a deep breath and drawing in the baby's sweet all-but-newborn scent, was that Cheyenne was safe.

"If these murderers didn't get Cheyenne, who were they after?" Catherine asked.

"Oh, don't fool yourselves—they were after your baby, all right, Ms. Amanda. But what they got was Avery Garth—his baby," the chief concluded, pointing a finger at Trevor.

Amanda, who was still holding her daughter as if she

never intended on letting the little girl go, struggled to establish a sense of peace.

Though for the most part it was still eluding her, she looked toward Trevor. "They kidnapped your baby girl?" she asked, utterly stunned.

Before he could acknowledge her question or tell her that, with all due respect, it was none of her business how anything involving his personal life went down, Gabby took the initiative—and the blame.

"I put Avery down for her nap in Cheyenne's crib in the nursery." Because both Mathilda—still sobbing— and Amanda looked at her as if she'd just turned feeble-minded, she felt compelled to explain herself. "Cheyenne had already taken her nap, and I thought the surroundings in the nursery might be nicer for Avery."

"Well, that was a damn fool thought," Jethro said sharply to his youngest.

"It's an *infant*." Darla Colton, Jethro's ex-wife, felt compelled to add her two cents. Every time there was some sort of an argument Darla and/or one of her two less-than-savory adult children could be found at the heart of it, fanning the flames. "It can't tell the difference between an embroidered pillow and a pile of hay," the woman insisted as she looked at Gabby. "They barely know which end is up at that age. Now I—"

"You certainly know which end is up, don't you, Mom?" Tawny interjected her two cents' worth with a less-than-pleasant laugh. "You always made sure to keep that end up, too, didn't you, Mom?" the young woman asked, taunting her.

A malevolent look slipped into Darla's eyes. "That's enough," Darla snapped at her daughter. She clearly needed more information in order to figure out which side to successfully play.

Rather than answer her mother, Tawny merely inclined her head.

Dislike glowed in Gabby's eyes. Why did her father insist on keeping this woman with her annoying offspring on the premises? Any promise he'd made to the gold digger was long since nullified by time. Someone needed to do a little housecleaning and get rid of annoyingly insidious people.

"It was a mistake," Gabby spoke up, owning her error. "And I'm the one who made it. Because of me, Trevor's daughter was kidnapped."

"I know, I know, but we'll get her back once the kidnappers realize they got the wrong baby. They just couldn't be heartless enough to hurt her. In the meantime," Amanda added, lowering her voice, "you did inadvertently save Cheyenne," she said with gratitude shining in her eyes. She leaned over and kissed her sister's cheek.

Gabby tried valiantly to muster a smile in response, but deep down, all she could think of was that, although she'd inadvertently kept Cheyenne out of harm's way, by the same token, she had placed Avery in its direct path.

The one did *not* blot out or balance the other. There was still an infant out there in serious danger because of her.

Chapter 5

"Well, I don't know about anyone else, but I think I need a drink," Darla Colton announced to no one in particular as the mounting tension within the room became almost overwhelming. Turning, she began to head toward the liquor cabinet in the living room.

"You *always* think you need a drink," Jethro bit off as he glared at his ex-wife. "Matter of fact, I never knew a time when you didn't."

Darla turned back to look at the man she'd spent one inglorious year with. She tossed her head indignantly. Her artificially vivid strawberry-blond hair swayed about her perfectly made-up face. It was said that she didn't wear her sins upon her face, so the years appeared to have been kind to her. She was still an attractive woman.

"I don't have to stay here and take this abuse," she snapped at Jethro.

"No," Jethro agreed wholeheartedly, his eyes shooting daggers at her, "you don't. You can just pack up and leave anytime—and that goes for those two leeches of yours." Since the first day of their divorce, it was what he'd been hoping for. But given she wouldn't budge, he could make her life as miserable as possible. She almost seemed to enjoy their mutual disdain.

The expression on the woman's face grew almost dangerously malicious even though her lips curved in a smile that never reached her eyes. It was the sort of expression that sent icy chills into the heart of the recipient. Most of the time, Jethro was immune.

"You *really* wouldn't want me to do that, Jethro," she warned "sweetly." "Because I'll be leaving one hell of a parting gift in my wake."

It was a threat—not the first—and everyone within hearing range took note of it except for the chief. It wasn't that Drucker hadn't heard; it was a case of hearing the threat far too often, to the point of being anesthetized to it.

But whatever it was that Darla was rumored to have to hold over Jethro's head, that problem existed between Jethro and his ex, and it was none of his concern right now. Faye's murder and the subsequent kidnapping of the Garth baby was priority number one.

The chief glanced over toward the head housekeeper. Her gut-wrenching wails had toned down into something like pronounced sobs. His eyes met hers and he waited for a beat, until the sobs subsided as well.

Drucker inclined his head, indicating that enough was enough.

Taking in a few deep breaths, and barely covering up the glare she spared the chief, the woman looked toward the stairs. "I've got to go see her," Mathilda told the person, a maid, closest to her.

"Can't let you go up there just yet, Ma—Ms. Perkins," the chief said, quickly correcting his slip of the tongue. He moved in front of the woman to block her path up the stairs. "The medical examiner hasn't gotten here yet, and he needs to make his preliminary findings first."

"After he does, *then* can I see her?" Mathilda asked.

The chief shook his head, looking just the slightest bit uncomfortable about refusing the woman's request. "He's got to take the body back to the morgue and do an autopsy on her first."

"What autopsy?" Mathilda cried in disbelief. "Why is he going to be cutting her up like she was some giant jigsaw puzzle? Don't you already know how she was murdered?"

Her question took the chief aback for a moment. "Well, it looks like she was shot, but we won't know for sure until—"

Mathilda waved his words away impatiently. "Shot, stabbed, strangled, bludgeoned, what does it matter? Any way you look at it, Faye's still dead." She tried to duck under his arm to gain access to the stairs.

Drucker was quick to block her path to the stairs for a second time. She had better moves than the two who were part of his department's team, the chief thought.

It looked to Trevor as if a power struggle was going on that seemed to go beyond the obvious. The chief, who had authority on his side, seemed to be hesitant about establishing that point with the distraught housekeeper. Mathilda did have an intimidating quality about her when she dealt with the staff, but Drucker, after all, was the chief of police. That was supposed to trump any sort of minor dictatorial power the housekeeper could exert.

"It might make a difference in finding her killer," Trevor pointed out. "And the person or persons who took Avery."

Mathilda hardly seemed to hear him. Her attention was on the man blocking her way up the stairs. She appeared entirely focused on her one goal: to get to see Faye one last time. She made it seem as if she needed closure.

"Faye was my best friend," she cried. "I need to say goodbye."

Drucker was somewhat frustrated, like a man at the end of his options who didn't know which way to turn to minimize the coming confrontation.

"You can say goodbye after the autopsy. I'll escort you to the morgue personally," Drucker promised.

She opened her mouth as if she was about to say something terse about his offer just before she rejected it, but instead, Mathilda surprised everyone—including, apparently, the chief, by saying, "You're right, of course. I didn't mean to challenge you, Chief. This whole thing has just thrown me completely for a loop."

Rather than take her apology in stride, the chief actually seemed relieved to Gabby as she looked on from the sidelines.

"That's understandable," he agreed. Moving back to the center of the room, he announced in a loud voice, "I know you all have other places to be and other things to be doing, but if you can all just be a little patient, this'll be over before you know it."

"Too late," Trip quipped, a sneer all but consuming his thin, bony features. His complexion appeared that much pastier because of his dyed hair, which for all the world looked as if he'd used black shoe polish to achieve the color.

His sister, Tawny, perched on the arm of one of the sofas in the living room, snickered.

Gabby, whose nerves felt dangerously close to snapping, glared at the duo. "I'm glad you all find Faye's murder such a chuckle."

A born protector, Amanda put one arm comfortingly around her younger sister's shoulders. The show of unity was clear. They might approach things differently, but at the bottom they were sisters—that meant being *there* for each other should the incident indicate the need.

"Hang in there, honey," Amanda told her, her words loud enough for the two under discussion to hear. "Those two aren't worth getting yourself worked up over even for a minute."

"Maybe little Miss Goody Two-shoes would prefer to get herself worked up over a big, sweaty wrangler," Tawny suggested, her implication abundantly clear. Her eyes washed over Trevor hungrily, with an air of entitlement that all but said that *she* should be the one receiving Trevor's personal attention.

"That's just about enough out of everybody!" Drucker declared in a loud voice. It earned him glares from Darla and her duo as well as from Jethro himself.

"How long you intend on standin' there, playing big-city cop?" Jethro asked him. It was evident that he had lost his patience with this game and just wanted everyone to leave.

"Just need to ask everyone their whereabouts from approximately— What time did you say you put the other infant in the wrong crib?" Drucker asked, turning to Gabby for his information.

The other infant.

Gabby chafed at the chief's unspoken implication, that Avery was "the other infant," as in expendable— as in easily replaced.

Had that been the chief's intention, or was it just a thoughtless oversight?

"Eleven," she replied.

Drucker nodded, continuing. "Between eleven and— What time did you find the victim?" he asked.

"Faye—her name was Faye," Gabby stressed, her voice cracking. The way the chief was referring to the dead woman—a woman who had obviously lost her life trying to save an infant—made it sound so clinical, so impersonal. She wasn't just some faceless stranger or some robot that had been brought down; she had been a flesh-and-blood person Gabby had known for a good portion of her life. A person who would be greatly missed.

"No disrespect intended, little lady," the chief said. "I know what her name was." He paused for a moment, still waiting for his answer. "The time?" he prodded.

She thought for only a moment. If she lived to be a hundred, she was never going to forget the sight of Faye lying there on the floor, her life having ebbed away from her as quickly as her blood did.

"We found her at two," she told Drucker.

The use of the pronoun confused him. "You went up there together?" Drucker asked, looking from Gabby to the man who had called him to come to the ranch.

"I was going up to check on Avery when I heard Ms. Colton scream," Trevor recited dispassionately.

"So you found her first?" Drucker asked, looking at Gabby.

"Yes, I already told you that," she insisted, trying very hard not to lose her temper. She didn't care for what she took to be the chief's patronizing tone.

"Just establishing the timeline for everyone," Drucker told her, looking around at the other people who filled the foyer and the living room. "Now then, I'll need to know where all of you were at that time."

"Are you for real?" Jethro asked angrily. "We already told you—" he took a breath to center himself again and only half succeeded "—we were at the damn rodeo. You want me to paint you a picture?"

"Verbal answers will do, Mr. Colton," the chief replied, clearly struggling to remain polite.

Jethro had only so much patience and it was long gone by now. He saw no need for extensive research.

"The woman's still going to be dead, no matter what conclusions your little investigation get you. Looks to me that she got killed getting in the way and the killer got the wrong baby, so there goes his profit margin." The smile on his lips was a cold one. "So it seems like he's already paying for his crime."

Trevor couldn't see where his employer was going with this reasoning—other than making it rather clear that capturing the person responsible didn't interest him. It had ceased to the second he realized that it wasn't his granddaughter who had actually been kidnapped. Trevor had always known that the man was a coldhearted SOB, but the pay had been more than good, and he'd figured that he wasn't a saint himself. However, this was a new low, even for Colton.

"And what's to keep him from coming back and kidnapping the *right* baby the next time?" Trevor asked.

The question caused Jethro to bluster, but he had no answer to it. With a loud, exasperated sigh, he waved the chief on, a ruler giving a commoner permission to continue with his tiny, hopeless little task.

"I also need to know if any of you gave a copy of the house keys to anyone." When more than a few hands went up in response to the question, Drucker glanced over toward Trevor. "You feel like giving me a hand here, Garth?" And then, because he wasn't completely devoid of compassion, he asked, "Or would you rather sit this one out because it's your—"

Drucker never got a chance to finish. Trevor pointed toward the group of people standing by the bay window, all of them too wound up to attempt to relax and try to pace themselves a little. "I'll take this group— you take the others."

It was exactly what he'd been thinking. "Sounds like a plan," Drucker agreed.

Stepping up before the chief began talking to the first group, Gabby asked him, "What can I do?" She needed to find some way to help get Avery back. Only then would she be able to function like a person again. Until then, she was completely wrapped up in guilt and concern.

Overhearing, Trevor spared her a withering look. "You can go sit over there," he said, indicating a chair on the far side of the living room.

She didn't even have to look where he was pointing. She knew he wanted to banish her. She supposed she couldn't exactly blame him.

"But I want to help," she insisted.

Trevor had very little patience and none to spend on her. "Don't you think that you've done enough?" he pointed out coldly.

Before she could attempt to answer him, there was a hard knock at the front door.

Because the doorknob gave under the pressure of

his turning it, the man who had knocked pushed the door open slowly.

The medical examiner, along with his youthful aide, who looked as though he were barely old enough to shave and had only just now mastered the ability to push a gurney before him without managing to bump up against the medical examiner's back.

"Someone said something about a body?" the M.E. asked cheerfully.

This, Gabby thought, was going to be a very rough, long day.

Trevor curled his fingers into his hands, clenching them at his sides in sheer frustration.

Two hours of questioning had yielded nothing.

Like it or not, everyone seemed to have an alibi for the time frame that had seen Faye's demise. They were all at the rodeo—or claimed to be.

Several of the staff served as alibis for one another, but there were other alibis that still required verification, and that, Trevor knew, was going to require a bit of time—something that he felt they didn't have and that they were steadily running out of in this case.

Most kidnapping victims died within the first thirty-six hours.

He had to find Avery!

It was the one driving thought—the *only* thought—that seemed to give him the will to go on. He needed to for Avery's sake.

Having temporarily hit the wall at this point, he cast

about for something that would recharge him before he returned to his search for Avery.

Toward that end, he acknowledged another chore that had just been laid at his feet. One, he was aware, he could easily get out of if he wanted to. The chief had already told him that he was willing to be the bearer of the news.

But shrugging off this particular duty was the coward's way out, and painful or not, it was a responsibility Trevor felt he had a duty to shoulder. He was not, nor had he ever been, a man who passed the buck.

Dylan Frick deserved to hear about his mother's death from someone who cared about Faye.

In a way, he supposed they were like brothers, he and Dylan. Not because of any bloodlines—Dylan was the governess's son while he had been her ward, her foster son. But blood or not, he and Dylan had spent their adolescent years together, raised, cared for and looked after by the same woman, the one they both adored.

Dylan needed to hear about her murder from someone who felt the event was more than just an antiseptic occurrence that had nothing to do with his actual life.

Dylan, who some on the staff viewed and referred to as an animal whisperer, was currently working at the rodeo for some extra money. For the most part, though, he worked on the ranch, handling the horses and doing whatever needed being done.

Turning his back on Gabby, Trevor strode out of the living room.

The moment he did, Gabby immediately followed

him. Since the area was still crowded with people, she only managed to catch up to him just at the front door.

Trevor spared her a look that would have frosted most people's toes. "Where do you think you're going?" he asked icily.

He sounds so angry, she thought. Not that she blamed him, but she still wished he wouldn't glare at her like that. She hadn't put Avery in harm's way on purpose. It was a horrible accident.

"With you," she answered.

"Oh, no, you're not," he cried. "You're staying here," he ordered, waving his hand around the foyer, as if a little bit of magic was all that was needed to transform the situation.

Stubbornly, Gabby held her ground, surprising Trevor even though he gave no indication. "You're going to need help," she insisted.

Not if it meant taking help from her, he thought.

"No, I am not," he replied tersely, being just as stubborn as she was.

She threw in her only card. "I'm willing to do anything you need me to."

He shook his head, a sliver of a smile rising to his lips despite the dire situation haunting him. "Do you have *any* idea what kind of a leading statement you just uttered?"

She could feel heat climbing up her cheeks—God, but she really did hate being so fair.

"I'm talking to you. I figure you'll take it in the spirit

it was said," she told him. "No matter what you say, you're a true gentleman."

Whether she meant that as a terrible future curse or a rare compliment, he didn't know.

Even though she shackled him with her innocence, he still frowned at her. "I've got to find my daughter. I don't have time to babysit you."

"Nobody's asking you to. I can be a help. I *can*," she insisted when he looked at her unconvinced. "Where are you going?" she asked.

"To the rodeo."

That didn't make any sense. Unless... "You have a lead?" she asked, lowering her voice.

"I'm going to see Dylan and tell him his mother's dead," he informed her. "That's not a lead—that's a death sentence for his soul. You still want to come along?" he asked mockingly. Trevor was rather certain that his self-appointed task would make her back off.

Trevor was too direct and someone needed to soften the blow a little. Gabby figured she was elected. "Yes, I do," she replied firmly, managing to take the man completely by surprise.

Chapter 6

Trevor looked at the tall, willowy redhead for a long moment, wondering what sort of angle the youngest of the Colton sisters was playing.

But as one moment stretched into another, it began to dawn on him that Gabriella Colton wasn't playing *any* angle. She really did just want to help. He supposed that it went hand in hand with her do-gooder attitude.

Either that, or she thought that, somehow, coming along with him in order to tell Dylan what had happened to his mother would make her feel less guilty that Avery had been kidnapped.

They both knew it wouldn't.

"This isn't something you can just stick a Band-Aid on," he told her grimly.

The news was going to be hard enough to break—

and hard enough to take. He doubted that Dylan was going to want an audience around when he found out about his mother's murder, even if that audience had a familiar face.

"I wasn't planning to 'stick a Band-Aid on it,'" she informed him. For a second, he saw sparks in her green eyes, but then after a moment they faded. If she experienced a flare of temper, she had it sufficiently under control. "I just thought he might want some sympathy, and frankly," she told him honestly, "I'm not really sure that you're capable of giving it to him right now."

Trevor scowled at her, thinking she was making a snide reference to his distant attitude. Where the hell did she get off, passing judgment on him like that? "And why's that?" he asked.

Did she have to spell it out for him—or was he just trying to rub her nose in it again? How many different ways could she tell him she was sorry? "Because you're dealing with your own problem right now, with having your daughter kidnapped and trying to get her back."

"And just what's in this for you?" Trevor pressed. "Dispense a little sympathy, feel good about yourself? Is that how it works?"

Was this making him feel better? she couldn't help wondering. Did he get some sort of relief by making her feel even guiltier than she already did? Did he actually *need* to hear her say how sorry she was and how bad she felt again?

Okay, Gabby decided, so be it. "Right now, I feel very responsible for what's happened to Avery, so no, this isn't to make me feel good about myself. That's not going to happen until we get Avery back and probably not even then. But I can certainly show a man who's just lost his mother some compassion."

"And I can't?" he asked darkly.

They had come full circle. Gabby raised her head, refusing to look away. Refusing to show Trevor that he was unnerving her. "No offense, but no, you can't."

He'd expected her to crumble under the weight of his anger—and his terror for the little baby he'd barely got to know. Trevor felt renewed respect. "I'm as compassionate as the next guy."

"Possibly," Gabby allowed. "If the 'next guy' happens to be a robot." When her assessment of the limitations of his compassion earned her a glare, she told the somber-faced head of security, "Sorry, but that's how I see it. You're a lot of things, Trevor Garth, and you have a great many things going for you, but you do *not* ooze compassion, no matter what you think to the contrary. If my being there can help Dylan cope with the news even a little bit better, then I'm going with you—and you really can't stop me."

There was no room for argument on this with her. She obviously intended to remain firm.

Trevor shrugged, not about to waste his time or his breath. She was, after all, one of the boss's daughters. "Suit yourself," he told her in a voice that couldn't have sounded more disinterested.

But silently, Trevor had to admit to himself that he really did like her spirit. That's twice she'd gone up against him and defied his instructions. Twice they'd gone head to head and she hadn't backed off. A woman like that bore watching—and from where he was standing, that wasn't exactly a hardship to undertake.

Focusing back on Dylan and the news he was bringing to the man, Trevor quickened his pace to his truck. He wanted to get this over with even as he was dreading the actual interaction.

The relatively short trip from the ranch to the site of the rodeo was made that much longer by the silence within the hub of the truck. Silence that seemed to somehow elongate the miles and the time spent driving them. But finally, they arrived at the rodeo grounds.

Without a show or any competition going on, the area appeared almost eerily deserted.

"Where is everyone?" Gabby murmured, looking around.

He could feel Gabby tensing up beside him in the 4x4. "Told you not to come," he said, interpreting her body language. The woman must be having second thoughts. And he couldn't blame her one bit. He dreaded every bit of this investigation—and what they would find at the end.

"That doesn't have anything to do with it," she informed him, dismissing his implication. What they were about to do had nothing to do with the way she felt. He had no way of knowing why she was reacting to her surroundings this way.

He didn't believe her, but out of curiosity to see just

how far she was willing to go in order to sustain a lie, he asked, "Then what does?"

Her answer wasn't what he expected.

"This rodeo." With no people milling around, the rodeo was stripped down to its lowest level, like an aging, once beautiful prom queen whose makeup had faded and was badly in need of a touch-up. "I really hate rodeos."

Trevor laughed, thinking she was making some kind of a lame joke. When he realized she was serious, he looked at her skeptically. "That's almost un-American."

It was her turn to shrug carelessly.

He took it to mean that she wasn't bothered by the label he'd temporarily affixed to her.

"Why do you hate rodeos?" he asked.

His tone demanded an answer and did not allow her to ignore the question. So she didn't. It had happened five years ago, anyway—just before he came to be their head of security. "Because Kyle Buchanan, after stealing my heart, decided to leave me for the rodeo."

The confession, coming the way it did, caught him by surprise. "Kyle Buchanan," he repeated, then guessed, "Your boyfriend?"

She studied a black mark on his dashboard before answering. "My first."

Trevor snorted dismissively at the information. "Thought you'd have better taste than to get involved with some guy who didn't have a brain."

It took Gabby a beat to realize just what her father's head of security was saying to her. That in his own way, Trevor Garth was actually paying her a compliment. Still, she could feel herself growing defensive over his tone.

"You don't pick who you fall in love with," she told him.

"Maybe not," Trevor allowed in an off-handed manner. "But you can either choose *not* to fall in love or to follow through with it."

Before she could find her tongue to take a stab at a coherent answer, Trevor had got out of the truck and called out to one of the rodeo clowns he spotted leaving the grounds. The man was still in partial makeup.

The clown stopped walking and Trevor crossed over to him.

"You seen Dylan Frick around?" he asked the other man.

Recognition filled the clown's brown eyes and his expression beneath the crimson makeup softened. "You mean Doc?" he asked.

"Doc?" Trevor repeated, slightly confused. "He's not a vet," he told the clown. "The guy I'm looking for works with the animals, horses mostly. Kinda has a way with them," he added.

Around the ranch, some of the hands referred to Dylan as a horse whisperer, someone who could almost get into a horse's mind, understand the way the animal thought and somehow manage to get them to do whatever he wanted them to do. For the most part, he assumed that it was a good thing.

The clown nodded. "Yeah, that's him. We call him

Doc 'cause that's short for Dr. Doolittle. He communicates with the animals," he explained. Then, to prove his point, the clown told him a story. "He worked with a horse that had gone lame. Rest of us thought it was the glue factory for Wyoming Pride, but not Doc. He worked with that animal day and night, and damn if he didn't get that stallion to high step proudly again. The rest of us at the rodeo just took to calling him 'Doc.' Seemed only fitting."

Trevor wasn't interested in stories or explanations; he just wanted to get this part over with.

"Well, do you know where I can find Doc?" he pressed impatiently.

"Not sure," the clown answered honestly. "But if he's not working, he'd be in that trailer over there." The man pointed out one that was parked close to a corral. Some of the horses were being kept there for the next series of events once the rodeo was under way again later that day.

Trevor merely nodded as he strode away.

"Thank you," Gabby called after the clown before she hurried to follow Trevor to the trailer.

Trevor turned to look at her, raising one quizzical eyebrow. Why had she thanked the clown? *She* hadn't talked to the man—he had.

Gabby could almost read the thoughts going through his head. "You should have thanked him," she told Trevor simply.

Now she was telling him what to do? "What are you, the etiquette police?"

She bristled at the sarcasm she perceived in his voice. But she was also beginning to understand that it was his defense mechanism, his way of surviving the ugliness he saw around him. He had to be deeply upset over his daughter's disappearance.

"I just believe in treating people nicely," she told him. "You know, follow the Golden Rule, that kind of thing."

He laughed again, shaking his head. "Yeah, how's that working out for you?"

"It's working out," she said automatically, then, because she was truthful, she added, "Sometimes."

He laughed shortly under his breath. Half of him, he had to admit, was amused and just a little impressed by her attitude. He couldn't help wondering what it would take to actually completely daunt this woman.

A part of him hoped that neither one of them would ever find out the answer to that unspoken question.

Glancing toward her again, he saw that he actually had to look over his shoulder. She was struggling to keep up with him. He knew he should keep going. With luck, she'd finally give up and go back to the truck to wait for him.

But even as he entertained the thought, he caught himself slowing down just enough for Gabby to catch up. She was abreast of him just as he reached the trailer door.

He raised a hand to knock on the trailer door. His eyes stole a glance in her direction. "Last chance," he told her.

Gabby knew the security head was referring to her backing away from the scene that lay ahead.

But this was going to be difficult for him, and she didn't want to leave him in a lurch. She was beginning to realize that beneath all that bluster and those scowls, there was a decent man who was just as capable of being hurt as she was.

And after all, the man was already dealing with having his daughter abducted. If she could help in any way, even minimally, she wasn't about to back off just because this was going to make her uncomfortable.

Despite her appearance, it wasn't as if she were exactly fragile, about to break at the slightest bit of jostling. Dealing with her father as well as the troubled teens she was determined to save, she'd managed to develop if not a really thick skin, at least one that didn't just dissolve at the first sign of adversity or a confrontation.

"Just knock," she instructed. "Don't worry about me."

"Stubborn," he muttered under his breath. Trevor told himself that he was glad she wasn't his headache on a regular basis.

She heard him mutter the word clearly meant for her and smiled to herself. "Yes, I am," she answered cheerfully.

"You've got big ears, too," he told her as he knocked on the trailer door.

Gabby was unfazed by the assessment. "I hear what I have to."

If he was about to comment on her reply, Trevor never got a chance to because, just then, the trailer door started to open.

Before it had opened up fully, Dylan was already talking. It was obvious that he was expecting someone else to show up at his door.

"I already told you, you're going to have to rest that bronco for at least today, maybe tomorrow— Oh." Dylan grinned at the two people he recognized in front of his door. He took his error in stride. "Sorry, I thought you were one of the cowboys I talked to earlier. Sometimes I think all that bronco busting rattles their brains. Even an eight-second ride is too much for them.

"C'mon in," Dylan invited, waving them in and stepping back so that they could enter the small, rather messy trailer.

When they did, Dylan looked at the faces of the two people who had just walked into his "home away from home." It was hard to say whose face looked grimmer. His smile faded away as he appeared to brace himself.

"Why are you both here?" he asked. Not giving them a chance to answer, Dylan followed up his first question with another one. "What's wrong?"

He turned toward the man who had been raised with him. They weren't exactly close, and they didn't really hang out together, but at bottom, because the same woman had been there for both of them, there was a bond between them that couldn't quite be dissected— or denied.

"Trevor? What's going on?" Dylan asked, more urgently this time. He could feel a nameless fear forming inside him, threatening to squeeze his insides until he couldn't breathe at all, much less breathe right.

"It's your mom," Trevor began awkwardly.

Dylan looked even more apprehensive than before, if that was possible. "What about Mom? Is she okay?"

All sorts of half-formed scenarios began to flash through his head. Faye Frick wasn't the type of woman to complain, even if she were in pain or suffering through some family crisis that severely upset her, at least on the inside. The outside always appeared to be cool, controlled, so he never knew how things actually stood with his mother.

To his utmost admiration, his mother always just seemed to forge on. It was her way because people always needed her. She was always in demand. And he had always been proud of her.

"Is she hurt?" he asked when Trevor made no answer. "Tell me, Trev," he insisted, then repeated, "Is my mother hurt?"

Trevor took off his Stetson. It was a sign of respect, and a chill ran across Dylan's heart. Why did Trevor think a sign of respect was necessary?

"Dylan," Trevor began haltingly, "there's no right way to say this."

He didn't care about a "right way"; he just wanted to know what was causing all this drama. "Just spit it out, damn it!"

So Trevor did. Unconsciously squaring his shoulders like a bodyguard going into the fray for someone he considered more than a client, he said, "Your mother was murdered."

Dylan didn't remember sitting down, but he knew he must have because suddenly, not just Trevor but Gabby as well was taller than he was.

A numbness had slid over him, but even now, it was beginning to ebb away as a really sick feeling in the pit of his stomach came to take its place. Dylan had always thought he could take anything.

He was wrong.

"Murd—?" Even uttering just a sliver of the word almost choked him. "Who'd want to kill my mother?" Dylan demanded in a completely stunned voice. "There's got to be some kind of a mistake," he cried, praying he was right. "She's just a governess, for heaven's sake. She doesn't have any money, any—"

"She died trying to save Avery from being kidnapped," Gabby told him, unable to watch Dylan struggling to deny what he was hearing any longer.

Dylan looked at her, the expression on his face a mask of confusion. "Avery?" He said the name as if he'd never heard it before. He had, but shock was making him draw a blank. And then he suddenly remembered. "Your daughter?" he asked, looking at Trevor. "Why would anyone want to kidnap your daughter?"

"They wouldn't," Trevor told him grimly. "Whoever kidnapped Avery thought they were kidnapping the old man's granddaughter."

"Cheyenne," Gabby interjected.

Dylan still tried to wade through his confusion and

shock. The Colton woman was talking about two entirely different wings of the house. Avery belonged with the maids and the wranglers, while Cheyenne had a silver spoon in her mouth as well as one in her chubby little hand. She slept in the main section of the house.

"Why would they have gotten the two mixed up?" he asked, then looked at Gabby, his voice almost pleading with her to tell him it was all a big mistake. "My mother's really...gone?"

Gabby pressed her lips together as a sob suddenly threatened to emerge. She nodded, struggling to maintain control over her emotions.

"If it helps any," she said in almost a whisper, "your mother died a hero."

Dylan stared at the opposite wall, not seeing anything.

"It doesn't," he answered. "Not really." He knew it should, but it didn't. All he could think of was that someone had killed his mother. And that she was gone before he could say goodbye.

That hurt almost worst of all.

For several long moments, Dylan was afraid that he was going to break down right then and there.

Trevor placed his hand on the other man's shoulder, a silent gesture of comfort and mute communication. "Hey, man, I can't tell you how sorry I am," Trevor told the governess's son.

"Yeah," Dylan heard someone with his voice reply. "I know." His desire for revenge, for vengeance spiked, speeding through him like lightning. Then he looked up at Trevor. "They know who did it?"

"Not yet," Trevor answered, then added, "But when I find out and get hold of him, he's going to be sorry that he was ever born."

It took a minute for Dylan to assimilate the information and what it meant. He raised his eyes to Trevor's. "Then your daughter is still…?" His voice trailed off.

"Missing," Trevor supplied as he nodded somberly. "Yeah, she is."

Chapter 7

Dylan followed them back to Dead River Ranch in his own car. With the horrific tragedy of his mother's murder so vividly fresh in his mind, the man told them that there was no way he could remain at the rodeo, at least not right now. He knew he wouldn't be able to give the animals he planned to work with today even half his attention, much less what was actually required in order to achieve any sort of hoped-for success. Gabby completely understood and had offered to drive with him, but Dylan had said he wanted to be alone.

As he and Trevor, driving Gabby back in his truck, approached the house, it was evident that the police were still on the premises, along with the county M.E. The latter's black van was conspicuously parked beside the chief's service vehicle.

"Wonder if Drucker found something," Gabby said, breaking the silence that had accompanied them back from the rodeo. Trevor had not said a single word, and just this once, Gabby decided that maybe it was best to leave it that way, since everything she said to the man seemed to irritate him to a greater or lesser degree.

It was as if her innocent question had tripped some sort of a wire. Trevor's frown instantly deepened as he told her, "One way or the other, I want a list of names of all the so-called troubled teens you've been talking to about this fool center of yours—and I want their parents' names as well."

She debated holding her tongue and just letting his order and his tone slide, but she came to the quick conclusion that holding her peace with this man did no good, and the emotional turmoil he was going through notwithstanding, she wasn't about to just let him belittle what she was trying to achieve.

"Look," she began slowly, "I know that you're hurting—"

"Hurting?" Trevor echoed incredulously, all but spitting the word out. "Let's get something straight here," he continued gruffly. "I'm not 'hurting'—I'm damn angry and really worried, to boot. If it wasn't for you putting my kid into your fancy nursery—"

Gabby had always prided herself on being even-tempered and levelheaded, but he was shouting at her and his anger sparked her own. "It wasn't 'your kid' a few hours ago. A few hours ago all you could think of was palming her off on someone else. Permanently," she reminded him. "Now, I'm very sorry that Avery was taken, and I swear that I'll do whatever it takes to find her and get her back, but all I'm guilty of is trying to be nice to her—nicer than her father was to her," she pointed out.

The moment the words were out of her mouth, Gabby felt remorseful and not because Trevor was glaring at her. This was an awful situation, and maybe *he* wasn't smart enough to be aware that he was dealing with it by lashing out, but she should have been. The teens she worked with had the exact same problem, pretending they were emotionally remote and removed from the hurtful situations they encountered and had to deal with every day of their lives.

Taking a breath, Gabby owned up to what she'd just done and said what had to be said.

"I'm sorry."

The expression on Trevor's face was extremely dark. "For messing up?"

She raised her head, refusing to be intimidated by the man she was with. "For yelling at you. Just because you're yelling at me doesn't mean I should be yelling back."

It was as if she'd just rubbed salt into his wounds. "I'm not yelling—"

"Okay," she allowed gamely, "how about 'expressing yourself loudly'? And if that *is* the case, I think you should know that I'm not deaf and you can lower your voice." She pressed her lips together, searching for a way to get through to him and still hang on to her patience. "We'll get her back," she told him, her voice softening so that she could sound more reassuring.

Her tone seemed to make no difference.

Trevor wasn't nearly as sure as she appeared to be, even though he didn't want to think of all the things that could befall the tiny girl who had no one else to be in her corner except for him.

"I'm not the cockeyed optimist that you are."

She resented the condescending tone and the label he'd just slapped on her, but she refrained from saying as much. Instead, she pointed out the obvious problem with the point of view he'd taken.

"Living without hope is very draining, not to mention daunting," she told him needlessly. "You need to hang on to something."

"What I need to do," he told her, finally getting out of his truck, "is to interrogate all those young punks you told about the bleeding-heart shelter you're building for them."

There is no arguing with him, she thought, getting out of the passenger side of the truck. She slammed the door hard, trying to leach out the bulk of her frustration that way.

It worked, but only to a small degree.

So did trying to reason with herself about Trevor's bombastic reaction to her attempt to talk to him. It was nothing personal, she tried to convince herself. It was just his way of reacting to a dire situation in lieu of showing that, at the moment, he was being eaten up by concern and worry.

In his place, Gabby thought, she'd probably react the same way—except that she would have done a lot less yelling.

Rather than offer any words of protest or try to convince him that the kids she wanted to bring onto the ranch had redeeming qualities she wanted to expand on, she just quietly told him what he wanted to hear: "I'll get you that list."

"Thanks," Trevor bit off without sparing her so much as a backward glance. Instead, he picked up speed and strode over to the front entrance of the house.

The scene inside had calmed down a little in some respects. Some of the household staff had dispersed, although the main housekeeper and several of what she considered to be her key staff members were still sitting in the family room, either waiting for further instructions from the police chief or, most likely, just seeing how this whole investigation into the murder and subsequent kidnapping would play itself out for the time being.

One look at Drucker's face as they walked in told Trevor that no progress had been made and no suspect as of yet had been found. If anything, only a few minor eliminations had occurred.

Nonetheless, Trevor crossed directly to the chief. "Any word from the kidnappers?"

Drucker shook his head. "Except for that note they left pinned to the pillow, no—sorry."

Trevor then turned toward Jethro, who was now seated in what was thought to be his favorite chair in

the family room. The old man looked somewhat uncomfortable in addition to his pale coloring, but that,
Trevor surmised, was more a function of the chair the
man was sitting in than in what was going on with this
investigation.

As for his pale coloring, that had been apparent for a
while now, Trevor realized. The man had been spend-
ing a good deal of time indoors lately. Not that it mattered right now one way or another.

"When the call does come in," the chief was saying
to the hard-nosed patriarch, "I think that you should be
the one to answer the phone—"

"Why?" Jethro asked sharply, interrupting the chief's
instructions.

Because it was Jethro Colton, Drucker knew that
he had to put up with the rude behavior. No one flour-
ished in Dead River if they locked horns with the old
man. So the police chief did his best to answer as if they
were just involved in a casual conversation rather than
something that could very well affect a little girl's life.

"Because the kidnappers will want to talk to the
head of the household since they think they have your
granddaughter," the chief carefully enunciated, taking
care not to say anything to offend the man.

If possible, Jethro's scowl grew even deeper. "But
they *don't* have my granddaughter," the man said with
an incredibly icy finality that Gabby found herself instantly disliking.

The point wasn't whether or not they had Cheyenne;
the point was that they had a three-month-old infant

that they *thought* was his granddaughter. An infant who needed rescuing.

"Well, they don't know that," Drucker reminded the scowling patriarch of the Colton family. "So when they ask for a ransom—"

Again, Jethro interrupted, this time with an even more detached voice than he'd used previously. "They can ask all they want—I'm not giving them one thin dime and I'm telling them so."

"Dad!" Gabby cried, horrified. It was one thing to speculate that he wouldn't offer a ransom; it was another to actually *hear* him say as much. "You can't say that to the kidnappers."

Jethro turned to glare at his youngest child. He hated being opposed, especially in front of others. He especially hated being opposed by one of his family. This was common knowledge.

"The hell I can't," he barked. "They're calling to get money for the kid they took, and it's not my granddaughter so it doesn't concern me. Case closed!"

"It is *not* case closed," she argued heatedly. How could the father she loved be so horribly unfeeling? "It's not your granddaughter, but it's still an innocent infant."

Jethro shrugged, his shoulders rising and falling like so many loose bones. "Lots of kids get snatched every day of the week." He pinned her with a look that'd had strong men quaking in their boots. "You sayin' you expect me to buy them all back?" he demanded, his voice thundering.

"We're not talking about 'lots of kids,'" Gabby

pointed out, her heart all but freezing in her chest at this display of indifference from her father. "We're talking about a single, specific infant who belongs to one of our own," she stressed.

Jethro's small eyes grew even smaller as he glared at his youngest child who dared to challenge him this way. "Are you feeble-minded, girl?" he demanded. "These people aren't 'one of our own,'" he insisted. "They're the hired help and they know that. I'm their boss, not their parent. If they do a good job, I pay them for it. If they don't, they're fired. It's just that simple, just that cut-and-dried," he informed her.

Gabby was acutely aware of the way the remaining staff was looking at one another and could almost hear their thoughts. This was building a great deal of ill will and animosity with the people who were such an integral part of their everyday lives.

She fervently wished she and her father were having this discussion in private, but it was too late for that. Still, she tried to maneuver him somewhere where she could speak to him without having every word overheard. This situation was already bad enough without adding hard feelings to it—not to mention that she wasn't about to see anything happen to Avery because her father wouldn't come up with the ransom money.

"Dad, could I talk to you in private, please?" she requested, nodding over toward a more isolated section of the foyer.

But Jethro remained sitting exactly where he was and gave no indication that he was about to budge so much as an inch. "Out here or somewhere 'private,'" he told her in a no-nonsense voice, "my answer's gonna be the same. I'm not paying any ransom."

For a split second, Gabby's eyes darted over toward Trevor. She ached for what he had to be going through right now, what he had to be feeling and thinking at this very moment after hearing her father flatly refusing to step up.

Her father undoubtedly thought that since they were in the midst of the staff this way, that she would just back off. And maybe she would have—if it hadn't involved the life of a child.

Drawing her shoulders back as if bracing herself against a physical confrontation, Gabby informed her father, "Okay, you don't have to touch a dime of your money. I'll use mine—"

Temper flashed in Jethro's eyes. "No, you won't," he told her.

Ordinarily, she would have listened and that would have been the end of it—but not this time. "It's my money and I can do whatever I want with it."

"Correction, it's not your money until your thirtieth birthday," he reminded her coldly. "Until then, I have control over it and you're not touching any of it without my say-so, girl." His tone left absolutely no room for argument on her part.

But Gabby was completely incensed at her father's callousness and lack of empathy. It made her wonder if he would have been willing to part with any money if it *had* been Cheyenne who'd been kidnapped.

"You can't do that," she cried.

Veins were beginning to pop out along his neck and throat. Had he been a dragon, she had no doubt he would have easily been breathing fire by now. It wasn't easy holding her ground, but she did.

"Don't you be telling me what I can and can't do," Jethro shouted at her. "Just who the hell do you think you're dealing with here, girl?"

"A heartless shell of a man," Gabby shouted back before she could think it through and attempt to stop herself.

At that point, clutching on to the armrests, her father pushed himself up from his chair, his complexion a bright, angry red. He suddenly appeared exceedingly frail to her.

"Now you listen to me—" he began, shouting over what she was saying.

Gabby started to out-shout him when her father suddenly made a strange, unintelligible sound, and then, with an utterly surprised and bewildered look on his face, he suddenly clutched at his chest.

The next moment, he went down in a crumpled heap just as his eyes rolled back in his head.

One spasmodic, jerky motion that involved his entire body and then he went entirely still. Jethro was unconscious.

The chief, who had just moved to position himself between the two participants of the shouting match that was going on, was closest to Jethro. Consequently, the law-enforcement officer made an attempt to grab the senior Colton before Jethro hit the floor.

But the chief missed. The man muttered a few choice words under his breath as he saw Jethro make contact with the tile.

Standing on the sidelines and looking on, Trevor was convinced it was all an act on his boss's part to shift attention from the argument over money as well as terminate it. A side effect of this would be garnering sympathy for himself as well.

But a closer look at the man on the floor told Trevor that this wasn't an act. Colton was out, cold.

Had the ornery old coot suffered a heart attack or a possible stroke?

In any event, the man obviously needed help. Swallowing an oath, Trevor pushed his way through the ring of Colton daughters as well as the chief. Placing two tentative fingers to the side of the old man's neck, Trevor was the first to ascertain that Jethro was still among the living.

"He's still breathing," he told Gabby. "Call the doctor," he instructed, leaving it up to someone else to decide just who was going to call for medical aid for the old man.

"Get him over to the sofa," Amanda instructed. As a vet, she had enough of a background in medical training to be able to render interim service while they waited for another doctor to arrive.

Though he loathed even to touch the heartless old man again, Trevor put his feelings aside and began to lift Jethro from the floor. Drucker stepped in to help carry the load, but Trevor put him off.

"I got this," he said in a voice that made the chief instantly back away.

The chief was overweight and utterly out of shape. All they needed, Trevor couldn't help thinking, was two possible heart attacks, back-to-back. That would *really* mess them up.

Gabby was already on the phone, calling the doctor as Trevor carried her father to the oversize sofa that faced the fireplace. She rattled off the details quickly, then hung up.

"Is he coming?" Amanda asked the second Gabby was off the phone.

"I don't know," Gabby told her honestly. "I left a message on his answering machine," she explained when she saw the look of impatient confusion on her older sister's face.

Amanda merely nodded, taking her father's pulse and doing what she could to make him as comfortable as possible even though the man was still unconscious.

Gabby was worried, upset, both over her father's sudden passing out the way he had and over his stubborn refusal to provide the money to ransom Trevor's daughter once the call came through.

Because of that, Gabby didn't immediately pick up on the whispered conversations. But after a beat, while Amanda worked and Trevor stood over her father, she became aware of the disgruntled fragments of conversations going on all around her.

Her father had managed to alienate his entire staff by his refusal to help and his blunt dismissal of the plight of one of the "help," as he viewed everyone who was not directly related to him by blood or by intentional design, such as his ex-wife and her two parasitic children.

It didn't help matters any to have Darla come rushing over, making an almost comical show of being distraught.

She was wringing her hands as she cried, "Is he dead? Is Jethro dead? Oh, I told him to take better care of himself, but he just wouldn't listen and now just look! He's—"

"Not dead," Amanda informed the insufferable drama queen very calmly, doing what she could to hide the absolute disdain she had for the woman who had been their mother for exactly a year before her father finally came to his senses. Her tone was cold as she told the other woman, "Don't go dancing on his grave just yet, Darla. He's not ready to be buried."

Clutching her drink—was that Darla's second or her third? Gabby couldn't help wondering—the woman peered at Jethro's unconscious, almost bloodless face and asked, "Are you sure?"

Gabby took a firm hold of the woman's shoulders and deliberately moved her aside. "She's sure," she assured the other woman.

Viewed by all as a kind, loving person who saw only the good, redeeming qualities in most people, there was still not a drop of affection in her voice as she addressed her former stepmother.

With a huff, the other woman shrugged off Gabby's hands, turned on her heel and marched away.

Darla was out of Gabby's thoughts the second the woman was out of her line of vision. Right now, Gabby had far more important things to think about.

Chapter 8

Gabby felt as if she could hardly catch her breath today. It seemed as though it was just one thing after another and it was hard to say which was really the worst of it.

A murder, a kidnapping and then her father collapsing in the middle of a tirade was practically too much to handle. She was afraid that anything more—large or small—would send her careening over the edge.

But the problems insisted on continuing.

Barely an hour after her father had been taken to the nearest hospital by ambulance, one of the maids, Gemma Harrigan, sought her out for a private word. The tall, angular young brunette was carrying a suitcase.

"Are you going somewhere?" Gabby asked the

woman. As far as she knew, Gemma hadn't applied for a vacation or any sort of leave of absence.

"Yes, I am," Gemma informed her, choosing her words as if she were picking her way through a live minefield. "I'm going away."

"Gemma," Gabby began, thinking that Faye's murder was what was frightening the long-time employee into a hasty departure.

But Gemma was quick to interrupt. "I'm sorry, Ms. Gabby, but I have to go. I know times are hard and I might regret this down the line, but I have to hand in my resignation."

"Your resignation?" Gabby repeated, stunned. This was worse than she'd thought.

"Yes, and I wanted you to know why, Ms. Gabby." The maid took a long breath, trying to fortify herself for what she had to say. "While I feel very close to you and your sisters," she began, offering a small, fleeting smile as she looked at Gabby, "in all good conscience I just cannot continue working for a man like your father. I cannot work for a man who had no sense of loyalty toward the people who work for him—and I'm not the only one who feels this way," the older woman warned Gabby.

Did that mean that more people would be quitting? Oh, God, she hoped not. All Gabby could think of at this moment was that she wasn't up to this.

Torn, Gabby felt tugged in half a dozen different directions at the same time. While she was still angry with her father, her concern over his health outweighed her outrage at his staunch refusal to help save Trevor's daughter. She wanted to be at the hospital with her father despite the fact that her two sisters had gone with him. But a part of her felt that someone had to remain at Dead River to hold down the fort in case anything else happened.

And then, of course, there was a large part of her that wanted to help Trevor find his daughter despite the fact that he had made it abundantly clear that he didn't want or welcome her help.

Since she was still here with the maid, Gabby did her best to talk the woman out of leaving, but it was like attempting to reason with someone who didn't understand the language she was using   none of her words were registering.

"Gemma, my father really didn't mean what he said. He's been under a lot of stress lately," Gabby told the woman, mentally crossing her fingers because she was making it up as she went along.

As far as she knew, there was nothing to say that her father *wasn't* dealing with a great deal of stress—why else would he have suddenly collapsed that way? But she had nothing else to base her theory on except for her gut instincts.

Still, she could understand why Gemma felt the way she did. Her father could be a very cantankerous old man when he wanted to be. She loved him, and in his own way, she knew he loved her and her sisters, but it was hard at times to hold on to that thought, especially when he could flatly turn her down the way he just had today.

Gemma wasn't about to be talked out of leaving, no matter what was said to her. The woman looked at her knowingly.

"Oh, he meant it, all right, Ms. Gabby. Mr. Jethro always made it very clear that the lines were sharply drawn between us. He was the boss and we were just the 'hired help.' Interchangeable parts with no faces, no names, no individual backgrounds that differentiated one staff member from the other. And, for the most part," Gemma went on, shrugging her wide shoulders, "I guess that's okay. But when Mr. Jethro acts as if it doesn't matter that he could easily save the life of an innocent child by parting with some of that money he's been amassing for such a long time—more money than any one man could possibly use up in a lifetime—well, that makes it time to move on, in my book."

Gemma offered her a sad smile. "I'm really sorry, Ms. Gabby. You've always been a real pleasure to work with, even more than your sisters. I hope you can find that baby—I truly do," she said by way of a parting last comment.

Oh, me, too, Gemma. Me, too, Gabby thought as she watched the other woman pick up her suitcase and then leave.

The moment Gemma was gone, Gabby wove her way back to the main wing of the house, feeling more than a little overwhelmed.

Well, that had certainly not gone well. She prayed

that there weren't going to be others opting to leave. She needed everyone to remain on board and go about their assigned business. She had no time to try to find replacements. Not when everything was being turned upside down.

As she walked, she took out her cell phone and placed a call to Amanda.

The moment she heard her sister's voice on the other end of the line, she asked, "How is he?"

"Gabby?" It was more of a confirmation than a guess on Amanda's part. She went on to answer her sister's question. "Dad's still unconscious. They're running tests on him right now, but no one's saying anything yet. Where are you?"

"I'm still at the house."

"Still at the house?" Amanda echoed. "I thought you said you were right behind us."

"I got sidetracked." Feeling as if her very nerves were being pulled as taut as possible, Gabby dragged her hand through her hair, trying to pull herself together. "I just spent the last half hour trying to talk one of the maids, Gemma Harrigan, from quitting."

"Judging by your tone," Amanda concluded, "you didn't succeed."

Gabby blew out a breath. "No, I didn't. Dad created a lot of ill will when he said he refused to release any money—his or mine—to ransom Avery."

"I know. It's not like he can take any of it with him, and there's certainly more than enough there to spare for something like this." Amanda sounded as disappointed in their father as she was, Gabby thought. Her sister's next words confirmed her hunch. "Makes me wonder if he would have taken the same stand if the kidnapper *had* succeeded in getting Cheyenne."

Gabby tried to reassure her sister—for both their sakes. "It's different with Cheyenne."

Amanda didn't sound all that sure. "Is it?" she questioned.

"Yes." Gabby *had* to believe that, had to believe that underneath, despite the gruffness, her father had a decent heart in there somewhere. He just got in his own way. "She's his blood. In any case, Cheyenne is safe and sound, so there's no sense in dwelling on what *might* have happened," she cautioned her sister. "Listen, I'll be at the hospital as soon as I can," she promised.

Amanda surprised her by what she said next. "Don't see what good you can do. He hasn't regained consciousness. We're just standing around, waiting for someone to tell us something."

Gabby knew there was nothing she could accomplish by being there, but she still felt she should come and keep vigil, at least for a little while.

"I can help you wait," Gabby told her sister just before she terminated the connection.

The moment she did, she caught sight of Trevor out of the corner of her eye. He was just walking by in the hallway and had automatically glanced into the room when he'd heard her voice.

"Anything?" Gabby asked eagerly as she crossed to him.

"Nobody's called asking for a ransom, if that's what you mean," he told her.

Anyone looking at the man would have said he was being incredibly calm, but Gabby knew better than that. She could read between the lines, and it seemed evident to her that his handsome, rugged face was more drawn than usual. Trevor was apparently just barely able to hold on.

"Was the chief any help?" she asked hopefully. Drucker had certainly stayed long enough, talking to the various staff members—making them all feel as if he suspected them of being the ones who'd pulled the trigger and had then handed the baby over to an accomplice.

Her question was met with a short, dismissive laugh. Trevor didn't bother saying anything.

"I guess that's a no," Gabby surmised with a sigh. Because she needed to talk, she told him, "I'm about to go to the hospital to see if my father's going to be admitted to the hospital or not, but I could stay here instead with you if you—"

Trevor didn't bother to hear her out or allow her to finish making her offer. Although he found the young woman attractive—more attractive than he was happy about—her father had made it very clear that there were lines not to be crossed. The Coltons were on one side of those lines and he, along with every other staff member here at Dead River, was on the other.

Maybe at some other time, he would have given serious thought to thumbing his nose at those lines, but right now, he was far too concerned about what might be happening to his daughter to waste time over such adolescent reactions.

"Your place is there, with your father," Trevor told her. With that, he walked away, hurrying off to some other destination he didn't bother sharing with her.

Watching him go, Gabby shook her head. For a little while back there, when she'd gone with him to see Dylan, she'd thought she'd made a breakthrough, but apparently she was back to square one with Trevor. He was just as distant, just as removed as he had been when this all began.

He was a hard nut to crack, even if his daughter *hadn't* been taken.

With a sigh, Gabby left the house.

She drove like a woman possessed, having little patience with speed limits that were posted in desolate areas. Their only purpose was to whimsically slow her down even when there wasn't any sign of anyone else on the road for miles.

She arrived at Cheyenne Memorial Hospital in record time. Armed with a room number that Amanda had given her, Gabby quickly made her way to her father's bedside.

Anxiety was her close companion as she walked into the room. She had no idea what to expect. The first thing that struck her was that the air within the room was thick with animosity and unspoken confrontation.

The reason for that became instantly clear: Darla had insisted on being there along with Amanda and Catherine.

But Gabby's heart leaped up when she saw that her father was conscious again. There were tubes inserted in both his arms, attached to monitors as well as an IV that was providing fluids.

For the moment, she saw beyond the punishing tubes and the gaunt face. Her father's eyes were open. He was back and that was the main thing.

Taking his hand in hers, Gabby struggled to maintain her composure. "Dad, you're awake."

"Looks that way." Her father's gravelly voice was weaker than normal, but his expression was as dark as ever as he looked at her.

For once, she ignored his tone. All that mattered to her was that he was awake. "You gave us quite a scare, Dad," she told him.

"Yeah, sure," Jethro retorted weakly. And then, because he found himself growing emotional, something that was completely unacceptable to him, he grumbled, "You were all probably hoping I'd croaked so that you could start dividing up the money."

"I wasn't, darling," Darla spoke up, all but sealing herself to his other side. She paused for a moment to dab at eyes that appeared conspicuously dry. "I was beside myself with worry."

"Beside yourself." Jethro snorted at the image. "You were probably just looking at yourself in the mirror after that third drink." He turned his attention back to his daughters even as Darla was sputtering denials. "I'd like to tell you all that it'll be a cold day in hell before you see any of my money, but the truth of it is it'll be a lot sooner than I'm happy about."

Gabby exchanged looks with her sisters. Was he just being despondent, or was there something going on that they weren't aware of?

"What are you talking about, Dad?" Amanda asked, then assured him with feeling, "You're going to be just fine."

"Easy to see why you're an animal doctor, because you've got no instincts when it comes to human patients," Jethro retorted dismissively. He glared at his daughter, angry because he was confronted with a situation he couldn't control, couldn't do anything about. "I'm dying."

While both her sisters began to protest that he wasn't, that his feelings were undoubtedly just the result of temporary low blood sugar or something of that nature, Gabby had an eerie premonition that her father's words carried some truth to them. He knew his own fate, but they hadn't been privy to the same information. What had the doctors told them?

"Dad, what are you saying exactly?" Gabby asked him. She studied his face carefully, waiting for him to answer her.

"What I'm saying," Jethro retorted, becoming steadily more agitated at the blow fate had dealt him, "is that the doctors said I've got leukemia—the kind that takes you out fast. They gave me six months, maybe less."

Gabby's eyes widened in disbelief. For a second, she felt sick to her stomach. She heard her sisters gasp in stunned surprise. "No," she cried.

"I don't pay them to lie to me," her father bit off angrily.

"Okay," she said, her mind desperately trying to sort things out and focus on a positive course of action. "There're different treatments to try," Gabby insisted. "It's not an automatic death sentence—"

"It is for me," Jethro said, cutting in impatiently. "I'm not going to spend what little time I have being a guinea pig, having them poke and prod me with their needles and making me puke up my guts."

"Dad, there are cures—" Amanda began.

Bitter, Jethro cut her off as well. "It's my body, my choice. No discussion," he snapped. He looked at Gabby accusingly. "Don't you ever listen? I don't *want* any treatment. I'm taking this like a man and you...and you can't..."

For the second time within the space of half a day, Jethro Colton slumped forward. When Gabby quickly attempted to help him sit up, she saw that he was unconscious again.

Darla instantly seized his hand in hers and uttered a swarm of endearments. "My baby, oh, my poor baby. I'm right here, honey. Don't you worry—I won't let them do anything to you that you don't want done."

Maybe it was everything that had happened today. Maybe she had just finally hit her breaking point. Whatever the reason, Gabby looked at her father's ex-wife and issued a warning. "You let go of my father's hand and back away, Darla, or I swear that I'm going to punch you out."

This time, however, Darla tossed her head and stood her ground. She hadn't managed to get to where she had in life by following any rules of decorum. She was a street fighter and proud of it.

"You and what army?" Darla sneered at her former stepdaughter.

Amanda moved to stand beside her younger sister. Her eyes narrowed as she uttered, "Guess."

The single word, coupled with a malevolent tone, was enough to make Darla drop the hand she was clutching to her breast. Muttering something unintelligible, she stepped away from her unconscious ex-husband.

Catherine had missed the potential fray because the moment her father passed out, she had run to bring a nurse—and corner a doctor if she came across one. She managed to find both.

Entering, she saw the way her sisters were looking at Darla. Something clearly had gone down. "What?" she asked Gabby.

"I'll fill you in later," Amanda promised as they backed up, allowing the medical team to have the access they needed to Jethro.

Darla deliberately moved to the other side, choosing to be away from her former stepdaughters.

For a while, bedlam appeared to have ensued. But, as with the scene at the house, the mood eventually calmed down again.

The prognosis the doctor gave Gabby and her sisters agreed with what their father had told them. He had leukemia.

"But you can treat it, right?" Gabby pressed, looking from the doctor to the nurses who had been called in to assist.

"We could try," the doctor replied cautiously. "And there might be a slim chance of recovery. However, according to our records," he continued, looking at the three young women and glancing at the rather gaudily dressed woman with them, "your father made it perfectly clear that he didn't want any treatment, and I'm afraid I have to abide by his wishes."

Frustration flared through Gabby's veins. This was completely unacceptable. "Can't we overrule him?" she asked.

The doctor shook his head. "Only if Mr. Colton were to be deemed incompetent by the courts."

Gabby exchanged looks with her sisters and it was clear what she was thinking. Desperate times made for desperate measures.

But Amanda shook her head. "I know what you're thinking but we'd never be able to prove that. Unfortunately, he's as sharp as a tack."

"No 'sharp tack' accepts a death sentence," Gabby insisted. "They fight it and do anything they can to get better."

"This is Dad we're talking about," Amanda reminded her. "Look, we'll try to reason with him when he regains consciousness again."

Gabby's natural optimism failed her when it came to that. "What if he doesn't?" she posed.

"Let's just deal with this one step at a time," Amanda suggested. "How's the search for Faye's killer and Avery's kidnapper going?" she wanted to know.

There was no solace in that department. Gabby shook her head. "They hadn't made any progress when I left the house."

It was obvious that Amanda thought her sister needed to be busy doing something and this was certainly a worthy undertaking. "Trevor's going to need help and you're the closest to him."

Gabby laughed shortly. "Depends on your definition of *close*."

"Look, the man needs someone in his corner right now and it looks like you're elected," Catherine said, adding her two cents' worth. "Standing around here isn't doing any of us—or Dad—any good, and you might as well see if you can accomplish something on that front."

"If we can pool together all the money we *do* have," Amanda suggested, joining in again, "maybe we can buy us some time."

"*If* the kidnapper ever calls," Gabby reminded them. As of yet, there had been no contact made.

"He or she will call," Amanda assured her. "They're just messing with your mind. It's called trying to get a psychological advantage. Go," she instructed. "And keep us posted," she added.

Her sisters were right. Standing around in her father's

hospital suite was just making her more and more anxious. She had to be doing something, making herself useful. It was either that or slowly lose her mind, thinking about all the things that were happening, things she couldn't seem to stop or change.

There was also the fact that a part of her felt so deeply for Trevor and that he needed her. He didn't realize it, but she was his only hope to get through this horrifying ordeal.

"I'll call," Gabby promised her sisters just before she left.

Chapter 9

"Anything?" Gabby asked as she quickly walked into Trevor's office and found him there.

She'd managed to catch him off guard.

For the most part, since Gabby had left the ranch, he'd spent the time allaying the staff's fears that there was a killer on the loose who was a threat to their lives, while trying to get to the bottom of who had killed Faye. If he found that out, he was confident that he would find the person who had kidnapped his daughter and who still, hopefully, had her.

He'd just returned to his office less than five minutes ago to make a few notes to himself—he always thought more clearly when he saw the facts written down in black and white. He certainly hadn't expected to have the youngest Colton woman come bursting into his office like this.

Rather than answer her question, he asked one of his own.

"What are you doing here?" And then an answer suddenly occurred to him. "Your dad's not—?" As much as he held Jethro Colton in contempt right now, he still didn't wish him dead.

"No," she cried, cutting Trevor off. After everything that had happened today, she really couldn't bear to hear Trevor ask if her father was dead. The very word made her ill. "They're keeping him in the hospital for now. He regained consciousness for a few minutes, but then he lapsed back."

He was trying to gauge her mood—was there something she was holding back?—and found that he couldn't. The youngest of the Colton sisters was not as uncomplicated as he'd initially thought. And she was far more than just a beautiful, empty-headed rich girl. He would have rather have it the other way. He wouldn't have been attracted to her if all she was was just a shell.

"But he's going to be okay?" Trevor asked, feeling that it was only proper to ask after the health of the man who ran the ranch and paid his salary. The fact that he thought of Colton as a cold-blooded SOB was beside the point.

Gabby blew out a breath that was more like a shudder. She was having trouble coming to terms with her father's diagnosis—and his reaction to it. Ordinarily, she would have kept his condition a secret, as she sensed her father would have wanted her to. But the burden of it was just far too much for her. She needed to share it with someone.

"No," she replied quietly, "actually, he's not."

Trevor's eyes narrowed. "Why? What's wrong with him? What did the doctors find out?" he asked, thinking that any diagnosis that had been ascertained at this point had to be premature. The old man hadn't been in the hospital long enough for any definitive tests to be run and evaluated.

Gabby's answer confirmed his feelings on the matter.

"They're still running tests, but during that short space of time when he did regain consciousness, my father told us that he had been diagnosed with leukemia." It hurt her throat just to say the word, and she could feel her eyes stinging. It was a struggle not to cry.

"Leukemia?" Trevor repeated, stunned. He tried to remember if he'd ever heard of anything specific concerning the disease's prognosis. "They can cure that, right?" he asked uncertainly.

"They can cure *some* strains," Gabby qualified, then added, "*if* they catch it in the early stages." And then she went on to say the most important part. "And they get to treat it."

There was something in Gabby's voice that told him the situation was less than hopeful. "They caught it too late?" Trevor asked.

"I don't know," she admitted, feeling helpless and aggravated at the same time. "My father didn't say.

What he *did* say was that he didn't want to be treated for the disease."

"What?" That didn't sound right. Who wouldn't want to try to beat a disease they had? "Maybe he doesn't know what he's saying," Trevor speculated. "When he passed out earlier, he might have hit his head and he's not thinking clearly right now—"

She would have loved to believe that—but she couldn't. She knew her father far too well for that.

"Oh, he knows what he's saying. My father was pretty adamant about it," she recalled as she shared the information with Trevor. "He said he didn't want to spend his final days being poked and prodded—and sick to his stomach," she added, paraphrasing her father's words.

Final days sounded rather ominous to him. "That means that your father probably doesn't think the treatment will take."

Gabby frowned. She'd never allowed herself to give up all hope about *anything* before.

Her optimism was obviously not a trait she'd picked up from her father, Trevor thought.

"I guess," she murmured.

"So what are you doing here?" Given the circumstances, he still didn't understand why Gabby had returned to the ranch. "Why aren't you back at the hospital, trying to talk him into getting treatment?"

Attempting to convince her father to take action right now would *really* fall on deaf ears. "Because the doctors said that my father is now in a coma. I can't talk to him and I can't just stand around, doing nothing." Her eyes met his. "I'll go crazy that way." It suddenly occurred to her that Trevor hadn't answered the question she'd asked when she'd first walked in. "Have you heard anything from the kidnapper yet?" she asked, phrasing her question more specifically so that he was forced to give her some sort of an answer.

"Nothing so far," he told her, all but grinding the words out. There was a measure of anxiety mixed in with his annoyance, although he tried to hide it.

"Don't kidnappers usually get in touch with the parents or guardians by now?" she asked, trying not to think about the very real possibility that somehow the kidnapper or kidnappers had got wise to the fact that they had the wrong infant, that *this* child was not going to bring them *any* money, let alone the hundreds of thousands they were undoubtedly anticipating.

And if they *were* aware of that, then what happened to Avery? Would whoever had kidnapped her just abandon the infant, or would something more drastic happen to Trevor's daughter?

The very thought, even if she didn't follow it through to its ultimate dire conclusion, chilled her down to the very bone.

"I don't know," Trevor bit off, using annoyance as a shield to hide the fact that he was growing progressively more and more worried about his daughter. Because of the note, he knew there would be some communication, but the waiting was killing him. Worrying wasn't going to bring Avery back. And, he had the feeling, neither would anything or anyone else. It was up to him to find his daughter and rescue her. "I haven't read up on my latest installment of the kidnappers' handbook."

He was upset—she got that and cut him some slack for being even more surly than usual. "So what are we going to do?" she wanted to know.

There was no way he was going to have her come with him. *"We* aren't going to do anything," he told her, emphasizing the pronoun she'd used. "But I'm going to go talk to those people on the list you gave me—"

"I'll come with you," she volunteered.

"No, you won't," he told her firmly.

The last thing he wanted was a distraction tagging along. Right now, he was torn between blaming Gabby for his daughter's disappearance and being uncomfortably attracted to her. The former was counterproductive, not to mention a waste of time, and he definitely didn't have time for the latter. The best way to handle both situations was just to not have her around. It was a course of action he intended to follow.

But Gabby had other ideas.

"Yes, I will," she insisted. When he started to tell her that there was no way in hell he was going to let her and her bleeding heart tag along while he questioned her less-than-savory candidates for the center, she shut him down with a blast of logic. "They're not going to talk to you, not with that attitude of yours. They're used to me and, to an extent, they trust me. If there's anything that any of them know that remotely has to do with the kidnapping, they'll tell me, not you," she informed him flatly.

The fact that she qualified her reference to the teenagers' trust, saying they only trusted her to a certain extent, told him that she had more of a realistic grasp of the situation than he'd given her credit for. Maybe it actually was better if he brought Jethro's daughter along.

Besides, as he saw it, he didn't have all that much choice in the matter.

"Okay," he allowed. "You can come. But I'm in charge of the investigation."

"Fine with me," she agreed. This wasn't about one-upmanship—it was about saving a little girl.

He had his doubts about the veracity of her statement, but he could hope. "Let's go," he ordered, heading for the front door. "We're just wasting time, standing around here."

"You got it," she said, eagerly falling in right beside him.

Questioning the people on the list she had written down for Trevor took the rest of the day. By the end of it, they still hadn't finished. Several people on the list were still left to question. But those they were going to have to see the following day.

Over the course of that time, Trevor had periodically checked in with Mathilda, asking the head housekeeper if there'd been a call yet. There was no need to specify from whom. The other woman knew exactly who he was talking about.

And each time she told him that there hadn't, his stomach tightened a little more, twisting itself into a knot.

And each time, just before he hung up, the housekeeper would assure him that, "Don't worry. They'll call."

But Trevor was far from certain that they would, and the longer he had to wait, the less confident he became that his daughter was still alive.

When he ended the call just before they turned around to drive back to the ranch for the night, Gabby could see by the look on Trevor's face that they were still left dangling.

She was about to ask him about it when he suddenly slanted a glance in her direction and almost belligerently asked, "Just what do you get out of it, anyway?"

For the most part, Trevor never wondered about someone else's business. But Gabby's determined involvement with this foundation to help a handful of inner-city teens had stirred up his curiosity to a fierce level. Why would someone like her want to spend her time and her money, not to mention her effort, on that kind of an endeavor?

He knew what he thought was behind something like this. But he wanted to hear it from her.

Trevor supposed that there was a part of him that was hoping she'd say something that would redeem the outlook he had about this sort of a venture undertaken by someone of privilege like her.

"Get out of it?" Gabby echoed. She realized that he'd

switched gears and was referring to her working with those kids he'd been questioning. He made it sound like a strict monetary investment for profit and she knew that couldn't be what he really meant. That sort of view was far too jaded. Trevor couldn't be thinking of her in that sort of light—or could he?

"Yeah, what do you get out of it?" he repeated. "Are you just slumming amid the 'poor folk' so you can feel superior about yourself? Or are you just trying to do something supposedly 'good' so you can stand back and make everyone take notice of what a 'big' heart you have, stooping down to give a helping hand to a group of underprivileged kids?"

Okay, now he was making her angry, she thought, trying to rein in her temper.

"What I 'get' out of it," she informed him with a touch of irritation in her voice, "is the satisfaction of knowing that because I helped a kid who would otherwise be doomed to a life of menial, insignificant jobs, they can actually make something of him or herself, can achieve their full potential and maybe, just maybe, be able to reach for those stars they could only dream about up to now."

"In other words, you want to be somebody's fairy godmother?" Trevor asked mockingly.

Now she was feeling a white-hot anger. What right did he have to presume that just because he'd been around her these past few years, occasionally grunting a greeting in her direction, that he knew anything about her? About what motivated her, what made her tick? He was being a jerk. And maybe trying to get her mad on purpose—or to distract himself from another very real crisis.

"What I want," she informed him tersely, "is to be somebody's path to hope."

"What do you know about hope?" Trevor challenged. "You were born with a silver spoon in your mouth."

It was growing dark, but he could still see her eyes flash in response to his statement. Almost against his will, he found the sight—and her—compelling. Her fire was drawing him in.

"What I know, Mr. Garth," she informed him, "is that there, for the grace of God, go I."

He scowled at her before looking back on the road. "What's that supposed to mean?"

"What it means is that although we can't choose our parents and I was lucky enough to be born a Colton, I could have just as easily been born to poverty." She might have looked innocent, but she was far from it when it came to knowing the kind of man her father was and had been. "Given my father's penchant in his younger years to bed any woman with a pulse, I could have easily been born to some poor woman who my father discarded the minute someone else caught his eye, leaving me unacknowledged and, more important, without the promise of any kind of a future."

She noted that he was quiet. Had she finally managed to get through to Trevor? Having got to know him somewhat, she had her doubts about that.

"That's what I think of when I see those kids who

have something extra, something special, and because of family circumstances, they're forced to drop out of school to help put food on the table and a roof over their family's heads. If you find that self-serving, well, I can't help the way you think. I can only do what I feel is right," she informed him.

Gabby saw the half smile creep onto his lips. Still angry at Trevor's presumptions, she shot a single word at him. "What?"

Trevor shook his head, amused and taken with what he'd just witnessed. "You're something to watch when you get a fire in your belly, you know that?"

She blew out a breath and let her head drop back against the seat's headrest. Gabby stared up at the darkened interior of the vehicle's ceiling. "I don't know what to make of you."

Trevor laughed softly for a change, rather than the harsh, dismissive laugh he normally resorted to when confronted with someone he viewed to be part of the clueless rich. "That makes two of us, Gabby."

She kept her face forward, pretending to stare out into the darkness, but nonetheless, she could feel a small smile of satisfaction curving the corners of her mouth ever so slightly.

She was making headway into the stubborn mule's territory, she silently congratulated herself. Granted, they were baby steps, but they were still steps and that was what counted.

Silence had returned for a moment and she took the opportunity to return to the question she'd wanted to ask before he'd gone off on this tangent regarding her foundation.

"No call?"

It was a rhetorical question on her part, meant to get him talking rather than bottling up everything inside the way he'd been doing for the better part of their afternoon and evening of interrogations.

"No." The single word echoed like a hollow sound inside the darkened cab of the truck. "They've probably realized their mistake by now and done away with her." His very throat hurt to say that, but he'd never been anything but a realist—and it had never cost him so much as it did now.

But Gabby was not about to share his dark outlook. "You just can't think like that, Trevor," she staunchly insisted.

"Then how am I *supposed* to think?" he demanded. He was just being logical—and it cost him greatly. "They took the kid, thinking she was the old man's granddaughter and they could get a lot of money out of him in exchange for bringing her back. If they're not calling, they *know* she isn't his. What other reason is there for not calling?"

She sensed that, on some level, he wanted to be convinced that she was right and he was wrong. Gabby's mind scrambled for a plausible excuse and she grasped on to a fragment of a thought, following it to its conclusion.

"Maybe killing Faye threw them for a loop. Kidnapping an infant is one thing. They take her, they give her back and no one's hurt except for my father's pocket. But Faye got in their way and they had to kill her—or, even more likely, they killed her by accident.

"But either way, they killed her, and if they're not professionals, which it's beginning to look like they're not, that's got to really be hard for them to deal with," she maintained.

"They can't just press a button, declare 'game over' and have everything go back to the way it was to begin with. They're rattled right now. They're trying to figure out their next move—if they can even think straight at this point." She turned to face him in the darkened cab, satisfied with her theory. "They'll call," she told him firmly.

He laughed shortly. This time the sound was not intended to be a put-down. This time, it was done to release a measure of tension that had been riding shotgun with him since he'd discovered the empty crib and realized that the daughter he'd been wishing out of existence was actually gone.

It suddenly occurred to him that the guilt he'd been laying at Gabby's doorstep belonged to him, not her. It was his, no matter how hard he tried to place it somewhere else. He'd wished Avery away and now she could actually be gone and remain that way.

"It's my fault," he said out loud.

It was almost as if he were talking to himself. Gabby debated pretending that she hadn't heard him, but she couldn't just leave it alone. She *had* to know what he meant by that.

"What's your fault?"

He stared into the darkness. "It's my fault she's gone," he said hoarsely.

Gabby studied his profile for a long moment, barely able to make out his features in the dark. He was serious, she thought. "Just how do you figure that?" she asked.

"Because I didn't want her. Because I wished her away." And now he regretted that from the very bottom of his soul.

Did he actually believe that? The man was more sensitive than she'd thought.

And he was also wrong.

"If it was as simple as that," she pointed out gently, "if people could just wish things away, I guarantee you that Darla would have been a thing of the past even *before* she ever got her hooks into my father and married him." The woman was a barracuda and everyone but her father had seen that from the first moment Darla came on the scene. "Wishing doesn't make things so." That was not a viewpoint that a pessimist would adopt, Gabby thought. "And you of all people should know that," she insisted.

He shrugged, still trying to deal with his guilt—and getting nowhere, although he did appreciate her efforts to talk him out of it.

Because she was trying to make him feel better about it, Trevor found himself warming up to her and decided to tell her *why* he'd shunned the role of father when he'd first learned about Avery.

"I figured I'd make one lousy father," he explained to her.

"You can't know that for sure," Gabby countered. "Not until you're actually in that position."

She was wrong. He knew. In his gut, he knew. Or he'd *thought* he knew. "It was just that I don't have the first idea about what it takes to be a father. I sure didn't have any role model to follow," he told her. Then, because she'd looked at him quizzically, he said aloud something he'd never told anyone else. "My own father couldn't wait to be rid of me."

Gabby tried to remember what she'd heard about his father. And then it came to her. "Your father used to work as a hand on the ranch, didn't he?"

That was the phrase for it. *Used to.* "Yeah. He drifted from job to job," Trevor told her. "When he drifted away from Dead River, he decided to leave me behind like so much dirty laundry."

Gabby saw his jaw harden in the sliver of moonlight that shone in.

"Just up and abandoned me without a single word." Up until then, he'd still tried to get his father to notice him, still tried to curry the man's favor. "I woke up one morning and he was gone. Faye raised me. Never said a word to make me feel bad about it or feel guilty because it was a hardship for her in any way. She just acted as if it was the most normal thing in the world to pick up the reins that my old man had dropped and take over.

"She let me know that I'd always have a home with

her," he recalled. "And I paid her back by getting her killed."

She didn't see how he could make that sort of leap. "Why would you think that?"

"Protecting my daughter was what got her killed," he realized. "Faye could tell the babies apart. She had to know that the baby the kidnapper was making off with was mine—and she probably knew that if the old man got wind of it, he wouldn't put up the ransom money." And that had got her killed, he thought. There was no way he would ever be able to pay her back for her sacrifice and it ate away at him.

"It was in Faye's nature to protect the ones who couldn't protect themselves," Gabby gently pointed out. "None of this is your fault," she insisted. "And she wouldn't have wanted you to think that it was."

But he didn't see it that way. Faye had made the supreme sacrifice for him—and he didn't deserve it. "Hell, even my own mother died on me."

"I'm sure she would have much rather gone on living and taking care of you. In any event," Gabby added, seeing that he wasn't ready to accept what she'd just said, nor would he allow it to comfort him, "she didn't just decide one day to abandon you the way your father did—and the way my mother did with my sisters and me," Gabby added.

The revelation surprised him and he looked at her. He decided that she was just making that up to make him feel better.

"Your mother died in a car accident," Trevor reminded her.

"Yes, she did," Gabby confirmed. "But first she left us. One day she just decided after having three kids that she wasn't cut out for motherhood—or for being married to my father, so she left all four of us, shedding us like so many unwanted pounds, and then she reembraced the single life.

"Unfortunately for her, it didn't turn out to be for all that long. But they didn't find any signs of remorse when they went through her things after the funeral. No regret for a rash action." She knew that she had cherished that hope—that her mother had regretted leaving them, if not her father—but hope had died a very cruel, quick death. "My sisters and I were expendable to her like unwanted baggage."

"If that's the case, then how can you stay so upbeat and optimistic?" he asked. From what she'd just told him, her thoughts, her attitude, should be just as dark, as pessimistic, as his were.

"I have to," she told him simply. "The alternative is much too bleak for me. I have to believe that things do eventually work themselves out, that good triumphs over evil and that the sun will come up tomorrow," she concluded, the corners of her mouth curving as she deliberately quoted a lyric from an old favorite show tune.

A lyric, she could see by the man's totally unenlightened expression, that was completely lost on Trevor.

But what wasn't lost on him was that, despite the

partial darkness within the cab of the truck, Gabby seemed to almost glow.

And there was something very compelling about that.

Very compelling about her.

Before he knew it, Trevor had decreased the space between them within the truck until there wasn't any—which was fine with him because he had no need of any.

At least not now, while he was kissing her.

Chapter 10

When he looked back on it later, Trevor honestly couldn't have said exactly what had caused him to lower his guard, to allow the tight rein he always held around his emotions to loosen just a little—just enough to let this break in decorum happen. To allow the feelings that he had been harboring and, for the most part, successfully hiding, to suddenly emerge and dictate this uncustomary shift in his behavior.

If Trevor had to point a finger at a catalyst, it would have been impossible for him to actually pick only one.

The reason for the break was embedded in a combination of occurrences. There was Faye's senseless murder, coupled as it was with his daughter's kidnapping, and, to tie it all together, he had come face-to-face with the brutal reality that the man he was expected to give his unquestioning loyalty and allegiance to had absolutely no regard for him—or his daughter—as human beings.

Even strangers could be moved to sympathy for another stranger if that person's plight warranted it, and what could be a more sympathy-generating situation than realizing that a person's child had been kidnapped and needed ransoming?

Moreover, had circumstances been ever-so-slightly different, it would have been Jethro's granddaughter and not *his* daughter who would have been abducted from her crib.

Given the weight of all that, plus the fact that no headway had been made in either finding Faye's killer or Avery's kidnapper, it seemed understandable that his defenses were eroded and his exposed soul was in desperate need of some comfort.

Whether he acknowledged it or not, Trevor craved solace and connection to another human being.

And Gabby was available.

The moment his lips made contact with hers, all logical thought ceased, at least for that isolated island of time.

And, as he gave in and kissed her, Trevor was surprised to discover something almost life affirming, something that stirred a part of him that had long been relegated to the shadows. Relegated there for so long that he believed it to be either completely dead or, at the very least, no longer functioning. Trevor *certainly* hadn't believed that his heart could come alive like this.

This flood of emotion—of vulnerability—ached for sustenance as well as encouragement.

She did this to him.

The kiss and what it awoke inside of him made him acutely aware that he wanted more. He wanted to taste her, to hold her, to completely lose himself in her and forget that a world existed beyond the boundaries of this truck.

Gabby and the simple act of kissing her made him want to cross lines, to feel things that had no practical value or basis for existence, other than existence for its own sake.

The solemnity that had been his constant companion for so long that he couldn't remember being any other way, for a fleeting moment, drifted away from him. For once Trevor didn't feel weighed down to the point that it was a struggle for him to walk upright.

Rather, it was now a struggle not to feel weightless.

The moan that creased the night air could have belonged to either one of them.

Trevor neither knew, nor cared which of them it *did* belong to. It was the unadulterated sound of pleasure, something he was basically unacquainted with and that he was now humbled to be allowed to share—whether or not he was responsible for the moan.

He did know that his entire body was heating up and causing him to seriously entertain the idea of giving in, of losing control and being happy about it rather than horrified or annoyed with himself for being a willing participant.

Shaken, thrilled, confused and just about breathless, Gabby felt herself responding to a kiss she'd had no part in initiating.

To say she was surprised to have Trevor kiss her would have been the understatement of the century.

After all that she'd been through today, a part was convinced she had to be dreaming. After all, she'd thought about what it had to be like to be kissed by this scowling, incredibly attractive man who seemed so indifferent to the sensual waves he seemed to always be generating.

Thought about it more than once.

Until today, Gabby had to admit that she had been equally intimidated by and attracted to the head of the ranch's security. But today's events had somehow managed to galvanize her, to harden her backbone and make her speak her mind rather than just quietly seeking to retreat if he scowled at her too hard.

It was as if everything that had transpired today had put them on equal footing: her father had collapsed and fallen into a coma, his daughter had been kidnapped and a woman who had touched both their lives, who had in effect had a hand in raising both of them and whom they both loved, had been callously murdered and permanently snatched away from them.

Sharing something like that *had* to change the boundaries around them, to change the rules that governed their actions.

And sharing something like that had to leave them, in their own way, both equally vulnerable.

That was the word for it, Gabby realized as the fire inside of her continued growing hotter and stronger: *vulnerable.*

Vulnerable to the point that she wanted to throw caution to the wind and take what was unfolding between them this moment as far as it both demanded and needed to be taken.

He'd started it, Trevor thought, so he had to be the one to stop it no matter how much he felt that he wanted her.

It didn't matter *what* was going on inside of him, what he felt, he was still just the help and she, she was the boss's daughter, part of the hierarchy to whom he owed allegiance. Given the present post that he held, he knew that he was even expected to lay his life down to protect her.

But anything outside of that was unacceptable, no matter what kind of feelings collided within him or how much he literally *ached* to possess her. To make love with her.

That shouldn't, that *couldn't* be allowed to happen.

So, despite the fact that Trevor wanted to wrap his arms around her so tightly that they would be all but impossible to pry loose, he forced himself to slip his hands up to her shoulders, and rather than pull her even closer against him, seizing his last ounce of inner strength, he pushed her back away from him, breaking at least their physical connection.

For a second, Gabby just looked up at him, utterly dazed.

20% OFF*
with code
THANKSJUL

Visit www.millsandboon.co.uk today to get this exclusive offer!

Ordering online is easy:

- 1000s of stories converted to eBook
- Big savings on titles you may have missed in store

Visit today and enter the code **THANKSJUL** at the checkout today to receive **20% OFF** your next purchase of books and eBooks*. You could be settling down with your favourite authors in no time!

MILLS & BOON

JUL13

Trevor took the opportunity to pull himself together— or to at least try. Several seconds went by before he could even locate his voice. When he finally did, it sounded almost surreal to his ear as he uttered a two-word sentence.

"I'm sorry."

Gabby continued to stare at him as if he had lapsed into some strange foreign language she couldn't begin to understand.

And then, when she finally found her own voice, she replied, "I'm not."

It wasn't the response he'd expected.

Trevor was convinced that the woman who had unconsciously stripped his armor away, leaving him naked and exposed, would grasp at his words, acknowledge what he was trying to do and agree that he should be sorry. Not only that, but he expected her to deny even the existence of those moments that had passed between them, tucking them away in a place where shameful secrets were amassed with the hope that they would expire and quickly fade away.

Instead, she blew that all apart with her own two words.

I'm not.

"You're not?" Trevor heard himself ask her incredulously.

Did she even realize what she was admitting to? he wondered, sincerely doubting that she did.

But when she firmly reiterated, "No, I'm not," it made him question his own conclusion about their possible pairing as well as everything else within his stark, all-but-monastic world.

Clearing his throat, unable to think clearly and deal with these confused feelings properly right now, all he could say to her was, "It's been a hell of a day. I think we both need to get some sleep."

There was no arguing the first part, but she differed with him on the second part. "I think we both know we won't get any," she countered.

Trevor had stirred things up inside her and she was fairly certain that she had done the same to him, at least to some extent. She knew that the stress they were under was partially responsible, but *only* partially.

Stress had allowed each of their carefully constructed veneers to crack just enough to release their trapped feelings. And that, in turn, allowed them to act on those heretofore untapped feelings.

It was a lot to take in.

For now it was enough that she'd let him know that what had happened was not off-putting to her, that she had enjoyed it and that she did *not* regret it.

The next step, Gabby thought, just as the first one had been, was up to him. She'd done what she could to let Trevor know that she was willing to have this thing between them go further—now the ball was back in his court.

A ball, she had a feeling, that would remain in play while they went on to try to solve the all-consuming, confounding mysteries that were surrounding Dead River and its inhabitants.

He started up the truck again, careful to keep his eyes on the road and *only* the road. "I'm going to get an early start in the morning, question the rest of the people on your list."

"I'll come with you," she promised, expecting him to give her another gruff argument, the way he had earlier today when she'd first volunteered.

Instead, Trevor just nodded and said, "Good." Gabby stared at him, both surprised and pleased.

Sparing her a glance, he saw a smile work its way along her lips—it was surprising what a man could see in the dark if he set his mind to it, Trevor couldn't help thinking.

He was unaware that his own mouth curved in a smile in kind—but Gabby wasn't.

It warmed her heart the rest of the way back to the house.

Trevor dropped her off at the main entrance to the mansion, then drove the truck around to the wing where he and the rest of the senior staff lived. Parking the vehicle, he went in.

Nothing had actually changed during the time they'd been gone—and yet, it had. The change within him was subtle. He realized that he was actually optimistic about the possibility of finding his daughter, something he really hadn't been when he'd begun his own investigation into the kidnapping.

The optimism was all Gabby's doing.

He hoped to God it wasn't unwarranted.

* * *

"Where've you been?" Amanda asked, relieved and all but pouncing on her youngest sister the minute she walked in through the front door.

Gabby realized belatedly that she had stopped calling either one of her sisters for an hourly update on their father's condition several hours ago. But she *had* told them what she was doing.

"Out trying to help Trevor track down his daughter. Remember? I told you the last time I called to check on Dad's coma."

"Any luck?" Catherine asked.

Gabby shook her head. "Not yet. We're still questioning people, hoping someone says something that'll point us in the right direction. So far," she told her sisters as she sank into an oversize chair and allowed it to all but swallow her up, "everyone's got an alibi for the time that the baby was kidnapped and Faye was murdered." She sighed as frustration took a firm hold of her again.

"Maybe it was some drifter," Catherine suggested, looking from one sister to another to see how the idea struck them.

But Gabby was skeptical—as was Amanda.

"A drifter who knew just where the nursery was located and that Dad had the kind of money that would make kidnapping a three-month-old worthwhile?" Gabby asked, shaking her head. "I don't think so."

But Catherine wasn't quite ready to let go of her theory—or to blame someone at the ranch for both heinous crimes.

"Even drifters know where the Colton ranch is," she protested. Her eyes shifted toward Amanda, silently asking for backup.

The latter was holding Cheyenne in her arms, as she had been ever since the moment she returned from the hospital. It was apparent that because of what had happened, she was exceedingly reluctant to let her daughter go or have the baby out of her sight for even a few minutes.

What if the kidnapper hadn't acted alone? Or had inspired someone else at the ranch to try their hand at running off with Cheyenne?

"I think Gabby might be right," Amanda told Catherine. "The few hands who were left on the ranch would have noticed a drifter and said something to the chief about it," she pointed out.

Catherine shrugged, surrendering. She sat down beside Gabby.

"How's Dad?" Gabby asked, changing the subject for now. She didn't want to get into a long, drawn-out discussion about nonexistent drifters. "Has he regained consciousness?"

Rocking her sleeping baby against her, Amanda shook her head. "No, and I don't know if he ever will." She frowned as she told Gabby, "The way he was talking before he lost consciousness again, it seemed like he'd just given up on everything."

Gabby refused to accept that. "Not Dad. If he had," she argued, "then he wouldn't have made such a big deal about not ransoming Avery. Even Dad knows you can't take it with you," she pointed out.

"Maybe you're right," Amanda acknowledged. "But all I know was that when we were talking about the kidnapping, there was this terrible look of sorrow that came into his eyes—"

"Maybe all this talk about kidnapping made him remember losing Cole," Catherine suddenly suggested to her sisters.

Cole was the name of the half brother they had never met. Born to their father's first wife, the boy had been abducted as a baby shortly after his mother had died. Their father had been hit with a double tragedy, which some people felt explained his present angry attitude.

Cole was never found. To this day, they didn't know if he was alive somewhere or if he had died at the hands of his kidnapper.

At the mention of the first kidnapped child, Amanda shivered and looked grimly at her youngest sister. "Certainly makes you think that maybe this branch of the family is cursed, doesn't it?"

"I don't believe in curses," Gabby said with feeling, although she was willing to concede that they certainly had had more than their share of bad luck.

"Neither do I," Amanda went on to agree, adding, "But there certainly is something about our family that attracts the crazies."

That Gabby couldn't really argue with. "Whatever happened with the investigation into Cole's kidnapping?" she asked, looking from one older sister to the other. She had been too young to remember how the story had gone.

Amanda shook her head as she gave a slight shrug, careful not to wake her daughter. "As far as I know, it went nowhere," she replied. "Dad certainly never mentioned it again."

"I bet it still eats at him, though," Catherine speculated. "How could it not?"

Amanda took it a step further. "Maybe that's why he's given up hope the way he has. Maybe he feels he doesn't deserve to live, not after losing his firstborn years ago and now almost losing his granddaughter."

What Amanda said made sense to Gabby. It started her thinking. Desperate for something positive to do, she came up with an idea. "Maybe we should try to find Cole again."

The suggestion was good in theory, Amanda agreed. But not in practice. "The trail's got to be at least thirty years cold."

"If he's even alive," Catherine interjected. She hated to think about it, but the odds of that were rather slim.

But Gabby wasn't about to be talked out of it. Her father was a gruff, exceedingly difficult old man to get along with, but she loved him, and if finding out what had happened to his firstborn made leaving this earth a little easier for him, she wasn't about to be dissuaded from this new quest.

"We've got to give it a try. There are more sophisticated ways of picking up and following cold trails these days than there were thirty years ago."

Since neither sister was shooting her down, she went on, her voice building momentum as she grew more excited about what she was proposing. "We could hire a private investigator, someone who specializes in finding missing relatives. If the investigation turns up anything, it would give Dad some closure. And we'd know we'd done all we could to find this missing brother of ours." She looked from one sister to the other, eager to have them sign on with her. "C'mon, what do you say?"

"Sure, why not?" Catherine said.

And Amanda shrugged, compliant. "It's fine with me, Gabby."

If they *did* find Cole after all this time, if their father saw that his son was alive, it might just be what he needed to rally him. Excited, Gabby almost clapped her hands together, but stopped herself just in time. She didn't want to accidentally wake up her niece.

"Great," she said, trying to rein in her enthusiasm. "I'll look into it tomorrow."

"Before or after you go off with Trevor?" Catherine wanted to know.

"During," she responded with a toss of her head.

Catherine laughed. "Got an answer for everything, don't you?"

Gabby's smile was wide and pleased. Despite the tense atmosphere surrounding all of them, for a moment, they all relaxed. "I try, Catherine," Gabby said. "I most certainly do try."

Chapter 11

Gabby couldn't sleep.

She knew sleep was eluding her not because of her hopes to find her missing half brother or even because she was so positive that she and Trevor could get to the bottom of who had killed Faye and kidnapped Avery. What was keeping her from falling asleep, even though she did her very best to talk herself down, was the memory of that unexpected, red-hot kiss in the cab of the truck a few short hours ago. Every time she started to drift off to sleep, she'd suddenly find herself reliving the whole breath-stopping scenario and she'd be wide-awake again.

It wasn't as if she'd never been kissed by anyone before. She had. And while there had never been an endless parade of men in her life, the ones she'd gone out with were all decent, good men.

The trouble was, none of the others had ever made her blood sizzle the way Trevor had, never made her soul sing the way his kiss had.

None of them had ever aroused her to such heights the way he had, not even Kyle Buchanan, the one who had abandoned her for a rodeo career.

She supposed, if she were being completely honest with herself, she'd had a crush—to a greater or lesser degree—on Trevor Garth from the very first time she'd laid eyes on the tall, dark and solemn-as-a-tomb man. Gabby could vaguely remember him as a young teenager, living with Faye and her son.

After that, there were years that he was gone, living in Cheyenne and working on the police force there. And then, five years ago, he'd returned, looking even more solemn than when he'd left.

As Gabby lay in her bed in the dark, she tried to remember if she'd ever heard him laugh with real happiness. Try as she might, she couldn't come up with a single memory. She felt that laughter was very important in a person's life. The fact that she'd never heard him express joy saddened her.

There was something about the man, something deep inside him, that reached out and spoke to her. Something that convinced her that Trevor needed to make a connection with another human being on an emotional level, no matter what he pretended to the contrary.

Just before she finally drifted off to sleep an hour

before dawn, Gabby decided to make it her personal mission to make the former Cheyenne police officer laugh just once.

Who knew? He might even decide that he liked the feeling and do it again sometime.

That it was a possibility worth exploring was the last coherent thought Gabby had before she finally managed to fall asleep.

"You look like hell."

The assessment had come from Trevor only a few hours later. He had come by to pick her up as he had promised and was standing in the foyer, looking at her a bit bemusedly.

The comeback was automatic. "Thank you. Right back at you," Gabby replied flippantly.

She'd had just enough time to throw some cold water in her face and pull on a light blue blouse and a pair of jeans, as well as her favorite boots, before Trevor had come knocking on the main door.

She felt groggy.

Getting only a couple of hours of sleep was worse than not getting any sleep at all, Gabby decided. In her opinion, had she just kept going, she would have probably felt a good deal fresher and alert than she did at this moment.

Gabby blinked, clearing her vision, and paused to scrutinize Trevor. Her flippant remark wasn't just flippant—it was accurate, she realized. Now that she looked, Trevor appeared to be in worse shape than she did. She knew why she looked the way she did and the reason behind why she hadn't got much sleep—but why did *he* look as if he'd spent the night wrestling alligators? Well, he did have a very good reason. Of course, he'd be up all night worrying about his daughter.

"I guess you didn't get any sleep last night, did you?" Gabby asked, still looking at his less-than-bright-eyed-and-bushy-tailed appearance.

Rather than answer her question, his natural suspicious nature had him asking, "Why?"

He hadn't got any sleep. Lying there in the dark, thinking, had brought out every concern he had, magnifying each one a hundredfold. That, added to his unintentional slip in the truck earlier, had made it all but impossible for him to get more than a few winks in before dawn came rudely bursting into his room, calling for him to get up and resume his search for his missing daughter.

"Because you look like you were up all night," Gabby told him simply. *Like I was.* Out loud she asked, "Were you?"

He knew that it was pointless to deny that he had been. The proof was obviously there in his face. "I was trying to figure out who was the most likely person to have attempted to kidnap Cheyenne. You realize that if he or they—"

"Or she," Gabby interjected. When Trevor looked at her as if she were talking gibberish, Gabby pointed out what she felt was obvious. "The kidnapper could be a woman, you know."

"Equal rights?" he asked with a sliver of amusement. These days, a man couldn't spit without it landing on someone who took great pleasure in insisting that women were still viewed as lesser beings than men. In his opinion, that was a crock.

Hell, he'd never felt that way himself. If it hadn't been for a woman—the brutally murdered Faye—he might have come to a sorry end years ago. She'd taken him in and saved him from who knew what fate. He had nothing but the utmost respect when it came to what had once been referred to as the "fairer" sex.

"Equal opportunity," Gabby countered, then pointed out, "It doesn't take much strength to fire a gun or grab a baby and run. And some women can be just as ruthless and coldhearted as men. More."

He was silent for a moment, then said, "You've got a point. Anyway, once the kidnapper figures out that the wrong baby was grabbed, he—or she—is sure to be coming back after Cheyenne." He looked at her pointedly. "You know that, right?"

She was painfully aware of that, which was why it was doubly important to locate the kidnapper.

Gabby also noted that Trevor had deliberately not said anything about what would happen to his daughter if and when the mistaken identity was discovered. He was avoiding mentioning that whole unsettling scenario, which could mean only one thing. Trevor had come to care for the little girl a great deal more than he was willing to admit.

"So," he concluded, "this threat really won't be over

until we get the son of a bitch." He caught himself before he began uttering curses in earnest. "I mean—"

She took his backtracking to mean that he didn't think the words applied to a female villain. Gabby assured him otherwise.

"The term works for either gender," she told him. "It speaks rather well to the lack of character. Okay, I'm ready," she announced, following him to the door. "There're just five names left on the list."

"The possibilities go beyond the list," he told her.

Which meant he intended to interrogate other people. Who? "Go on," she urged.

This was just off the top of his head. "There are a few new ranch hands at Dead River, men I don't know all that well."

Gabby couldn't help wondering if there was anyone on the ranch that Trevor actually *did* know well—now that Faye was gone. Outside of the beloved nanny, she'd never seen him hanging around with anyone. For the most part, Trevor kept his own company.

"And there's the boss's ex and her two spoiled brats," he pointed out.

She loathed all three, as did her sisters, but she didn't think any of them capable of murder. Or, in the case of Tawny and Trip, of moving very fast. Both siblings were the embodiment of laziness.

"You think one of them could have taken Avery?" she asked.

In a heartbeat, he thought. "Wouldn't put it past them. They all go through money like it was water, and none of them would turn down an easy way to make some more 'walking around money,'" he told her with conviction.

Gabby didn't really have to think about it. He was right. She wouldn't put it past Darla and her evil spawn to kidnap a baby and hold the child for ransom. Believing them capable of murder, though, was going to take a bit of convincing.

"Want to question them first?" she asked. "Most likely, they're still in bed asleep, so they'd be easy to find."

Trevor liked finishing what he started. "Let's talk to the rest of the people on your list first," he told her.

"You're methodical," she commented, closing the door behind her.

He didn't like being pigeonholed. "Just need something to look forward to," Trevor said pointedly.

Gabby didn't get it. "You look *forward* to questioning them?" She usually went out of her way to avoid contact with any of them.

"Grilling them," Trevor corrected.

Now it was starting to make sense to her. Gabby smiled at him. "I get it."

"I figured you would," he told her as he led the way to his truck. Under all that optimism was a sharp woman, he thought. He paused before opening the door to his truck. "You have any breakfast yet?" he wanted to know.

She'd barely had time to come down the stairs before she heard him enter. "I haven't even had coffee," she confessed. "You caught me just a minute after I'd gotten dressed."

Her words created images in his head without warning, and he caught himself wishing that he'd come over to her side of the mansion just a little bit earlier. Imagining what she'd look like without clothes caused his brain to all but fog up. Only exercising extreme control over his thoughts managed to banish the images—or at least relegate them to some far, dormant region of his mind. A region, he knew, he intended to revisit once all this trouble was behind him.

"Got some coffee and an egg sandwich for you in the truck," he told her stiffly. Belatedly, he opened the door on her side.

Her mouth dropped when she saw the bulking paper bag on her seat. Gabby stared at him as she got in. Picking up the bag, she could feel that what was inside was still warm. "You're kidding."

Her comment didn't make sense to him. "Why would I kid about that?"

"You cook?" She could see him, in a pinch, slapping a few basic things together, but an egg sandwich took a little creativity. The type of creativity that she felt he lacked. His skills lay elsewhere.

"I cook," he confirmed, then went on to tell her, "But I didn't make this." He nodded at the contents of the paper bag.

As he got in behind the steering wheel, she opened the bag and took out a fried-egg-and-ham combo placed on a toasted muffin. "Mathilda made it," he told her.

"Woman feels really awful about what happened to Faye. They were close."

The way he said it—as if it was a revelation—made Gabby look at him quizzically as she automatically fastened her seat belt.

"You didn't know that?" she asked.

He focused only on those things that applied to his job. A friendship between two long-time employees— even if one of those employees was his foster mother— didn't fall under that category.

"Guess I didn't pay any attention to it. Didn't pay attention to a lot of things," he added as though he were making a confession.

Gabby read her own meaning into his words, wondering if he was talking about her. "No time like the present to change that," she encouraged. Taking an appreciative bite out of the breakfast sandwich he'd given her, she nodded her approval. "This is really good," Gabby said.

He said nothing. He was too busy starting up his truck and deciding which of the people left on Gabby's list they were going to go see first.

One by one the remaining names on the list were crossed out. Each of them offered plausible alibis for the time in question. Checking out the alibis was simple enough.

It appeared as if the teens Gabby had picked to help because of their potential really would make the most of the opportunity she was sending their way.

And then there was only one more person to see.

The last person on Gabby's list proved to be far more belligerent than the other disadvantaged teens they'd talked to.

While the others they'd spoken to had all seemed a little defensive, they'd all had alibis to offer, alibis that were easily verified with a minimum of effort.

Pete Simpson, the last name on the list, seemed determined not to tell them anything beyond "I didn't have nothin' to do with any murder. Don't even know who you're talking about," he retorted. "All I know was that I wasn't anywhere near your precious ranch yesterday," the tall, thin teen who favored dressing all in black spat out.

"Then where were you?" Trevor asked. His tone was stern, demanding.

It must have rubbed Pete the wrong way. "None of your damn business," he informed Trevor angrily. "Just 'cause I don't live on a fancy ranch, you think you can pin this all on me?" he demanded hotly. "Well, think again. I'm *not* going down for this."

"We're not looking to pin anything on anyone, Pete," Gabby assured him, keeping her voice gentle, soothing. Her eyes were kind when she made contact with his. Her manner was the direct opposite of Trevor's. She was counting on bringing the teenager around. "Just tell us where you were yesterday morning from about noon to three."

It was obvious by the way he watched her that Pete held Gabby in high esteem. But he'd been fighting his own battles since before he'd turned ten and it was hard for him to trust anyone, even someone like Gabby.

"And if I won't?" he asked.

She looked as if it pained her to give him an answer to that question, but she did.

"Then we'll have to bring you into the police station and have the chief question you. He doesn't know you like I do and he won't be patient, Pete. It's your choice," she told him.

Out of the corner of her eye, she could see how aggravated the whole process was making Trevor. She crossed her fingers in her head, praying that he would keep his temper in check. Otherwise, all bets were off. She didn't know if she could undo the damage his temper could so easily do.

"If I tell you," Pete began cautiously, "are you gonna, you know, have to tell anyone?"

She sensed that might be a problem and tried to find an acceptable reason why that was. One particular one stuck in her head. "We'll have to check out your story with the person you name," she told him, watching his expression.

"Why? Don't you trust me?" Pete accused hotly, like someone who anticipated being betrayed—if he hadn't been already.

"It's called verifying your story," she explained. "We'd have to check it out even if you were the governor of the state."

"No, you wouldn't," Pete protested angrily, no doubt feeling singled out.

"Yes," Gabby contradicted him firmly, "we would. The law doesn't let us take anyone's word for anything without getting some kind of proof."

Pete's scowl was nearly as black as Trevor's could be. "The law stinks," he declared.

"Sometimes it does," Gabby allowed. Then, to balance it out just as the scales of justice balanced things, she said, "Other times, it protects you."

Pete blew out an impatient breath. It was evident that he was one angry young man. But it was equally as evident that he didn't want to go to jail for something he didn't do if there was any way to prevent that from happening.

"She's got a husband," he said unexpectedly.

"You're talking about your alibi?" Trevor asked the teenager.

Scowling at him, Pete nodded.

Gabby placed her hand on his wrist to get his attention.

She was doing it to create a bond, Trevor thought. Grudgingly, he gave her points for her efforts. She knew how to play this.

"We won't talk to her in front of him." This time, it was Trevor who spoke instead of Gabby. The promise carried more weight, coming from him.

Pete slanted a malevolent look in his direction. But a string of choice words did *not* follow. Pete was a foot soldier who wanted to be saved. So, having really no choice, he gave up the name of the woman he'd been seeing behind her husband's back. "It's Paula Baker."

She'd dealt with Paula once or twice, Gabby recalled. And, if she recalled correctly, Paula had a much-older husband. It wasn't an excuse, but it was a reason, she mused.

"Thank you. We'll be as discreet as possible," Gabby promised the teenager.

Confusion slipped over his handsome features. "What does that mean?"

"That means her husband isn't going to come and plaster your hide from here to the border," Trevor told him bluntly. "We'll make sure he's not around when we question her."

The wary look on the teenager's face did not abate, but he nodded and muttered a less-than-enthusiastic "Okay" by way of a parting comment.

An hour later, a very reluctant Paula Baker verified Pete Simpson's alibi in a voice that was hardly above a whisper despite the fact that her husband was in town, buying feed for their horses.

Thanking the nervous-looking twentysomething blonde, Gabby and Trevor took their leave.

"Well, that's the last of the people on the list," Gabby said needlessly as she walked back with Trevor to his truck. She could almost *feel* the minutes ticking away, but she gave no indication of her growing unease. Instead, she asked mildly, "What's next?"

"Next we talk to your father's ex-wife," Trevor told her.

She'd been thinking about that, about the possibility

that either Darla or her offspring were involved. "My sister said that Darla was at the rodeo." She'd forgotten about that earlier.

"Doesn't mean she couldn't have slipped away at some point and gone back to the ranch—or hired someone else to kidnap your niece."

"No," Gabby readily agreed. "It doesn't." She didn't want him thinking she was protecting the woman in any way. Who knew, maybe they would get lucky after all. "Okay, let's go talk to her."

"Don't forget her two brats," he reminded her. As far as he was concerned, they were all equally suspect.

Gabby laughed. As if she ever could. "Believe me, I've tried."

"Why does your father let them stay at the ranch?" Trevor asked as he turned the truck around to head toward Dead River.

That was a question they'd all asked themselves. "Personally, I think she has something on him, something that she threatens to expose if he doesn't let her go on living there in the style she's grown accustomed to." She followed that thought to its logical conclusion. "You know, if that's the case, Darla really wouldn't need to kidnap Cheyenne. She'd just use whatever it is that she's holding over Dad's head to make him give her more money or whatever it is that she was after."

That was true enough. "That still doesn't mean she can't get greedier," Trevor added.

"You do have a point," Gabby conceded.

"I usually do," he told her.

Silently, Gabby agreed. No use giving the man a swelled head, she reasoned with a smile.

Her smile did not go unnoticed. Trevor could feel his stomach muscles contracting, even as he tried to ignore the woman in the truck's cab and the eroding effect she had on his defenses. It was beginning to feel like a losing battle.

Chapter 12

"How dare you," Darla railed when Trevor began to question her. The almost anorexic-looking woman looked as if she wanted to rake her long, scarlet-tipped fingernails down his face. "How dare you suggest that I had *anything* to do with killing that poor woman, Faith—"

"Faye," Gabby corrected tersely. Leave it to Darla not to even know the name of a woman who was far more of a fixture in the Colton household than she ever was. "Her name was Faye."

Darla's eyes narrowed and a scowl turned her attractive, carefully made-up face into a mask of hatred that sent the lesser household staff cowering as they hurried away.

"Her name was mud as far as I was concerned. That

woman was always looking down her nose at me, like that nothing of a nanny thought she was better than I was," Darla fumed angrily, pacing around the sitting room of her living quarters at the far side of the mansion. There was no mistaking the fact that she resented being questioned about something so trivial as the murder of a lowly staff member.

Trevor's intense, dark blue eyes pinned her in place. Gabby was confident that had Darla had a lesser inflated sense of self, she would have been squirming beneath his scrutiny. "You realize that so far, you're painting yourself into a corner, don't you?" Trevor pointed out, his voice a harsh whisper.

If anything, Darla's haughty tone increased, reinforced by defensiveness. "I hated her guts and I'm not shedding any tears that she's dead—*but I didn't murder the woman,*" she declared, enunciating every syllable carefully, as if she were dealing with someone with a limited IQ. "I was at the rodeo. Hundreds of people saw me," she maintained with confidence.

Her father's latest ex was either innocent or exceedingly brazen, Gabby thought. At the moment, she wasn't quite sure which it was.

"That's because you were throwing yourself at that bronco buster," Tawny taunted her mother. Physically, the young woman was almost a carbon copy of her mother, albeit younger, a fact that both amused and annoyed Darla, depending on the situation.

"I was flirting with Travis—" Darla's lofty tone was tinged with annoyance—it was obvious that she didn't care to be judged, least of all by her own off-spring "—not 'throwing myself' at him. If you had any successful relationships of your own, you would have known the difference."

Tawny frowned. "Oh, and what kind of 'success-ful relationships' have you had, Mother dear?" Tawny sneered at her mother.

Trevor got in between the two women. "Okay, la-dies, sheathe those claws of yours, please. I don't need to witness a cat fight." He turned toward Darla. "These 'hundreds' of people who saw you, did you get *any* of their names?"

Her smile turned wicked. "I've got Travis," she vol-unteered triumphantly.

Travis was a common enough name in this area. "What's his last name?" Trevor asked, taking out a well-worn, tiny notebook. He turned to an empty page, then looked at her, waiting.

"Well, you've got me there," Darla confessed with a dismissive laugh that clearly said her word for it should have been enough for him. "But he told me he was rid-ing tomorrow, so you can catch him then."

"I can be her alibi," Tawny volunteered. "And she can be mine," she added, pleased with herself that she had brilliantly thwarted any need to question her regarding the murder of the woman she disliked simply because she disliked everyone within the Colton household she believed regarded her as an outsider. "We were together most of the time," she added.

Given a choice, Trevor wouldn't have believed either

one of the women, but the law didn't work that way, allowing him to pick what he wanted to believe and turn down what he didn't. Until proven otherwise, he had to believe that mother and daughter were out in plain sight. Of course, that didn't automatically mean that they hadn't prevailed on someone else to kidnap what they believed to be the infant heiress.

However, if they, or anyone else connected to the Colton household, *were* involved in the homicide and abduction, then perforce they knew they had the wrong baby. That would explain why there still had been no ransom demand—and could also mean that his daughter was already a casualty—or would be one very soon.

He couldn't allow himself to think about that. Gabby was right. To believe that would be to invite total paralysis to set in. He'd be no good to Avery or to himself that way.

Trevor cleared his throat. "How about Trip?" he wanted to know.

"What about him?" Darla asked suspiciously.

His patience clearly on the wane, Trevor asked, "What's his alibi?"

"Why, he was with us the entire time, of course," Darla informed him. Her implication was that he had to be a mental midget to think otherwise. "That boy wouldn't hurt a fly."

Flies, no, Gabby thought. *But people, well, that's another story.* As far as she was concerned, her former stepbrother had a mean streak to go along with his all-consuming laziness. Trip was actively working at not being employed in any capacity. So far, he'd been successful in his efforts.

Thinking along the same lines brought Trevor to the logical question of where did Trip get his money? The so-called allowance Jethro grudgingly gave the woman he had married in haste only went so far. A kidnapping plot didn't seem all that far-fetched for someone who seemed to be allergic to work, yet had expensive tastes.

Trevor was fairly certain that "Mama" was only indulgent to a minor degree—as long as it didn't cut into her own funds, funds she'd made clear more than once did *not* begin to cover what Darla felt constituted her basic needs.

"The entire time?" Gabby echoed, the expression on her face challenging the other woman's assertion.

Darla's eyes narrowed in response to what she obviously felt was her ex-stepdaughter's hostile, probing question. "That's what I said."

"Even the time you were flirting with the bronco buster?" Gabby pressed.

Rather than answer, Darla resorted to what she perceived was a threat. "Am I going to have to have my lawyer speak to you on my behalf?" She directed the question to Trevor, deliberately ignoring her former stepdaughter.

If it was meant to snub her, Gabby took no notice—or offense. "You have a divorce lawyer, Darla," Gabby pointedly reminded the woman. "He doesn't handle criminal cases."

"Then you *are* actually accusing me of having something to do with that horrible business?" she demanded, her amber eyes sweeping from Gabby to Trevor.

"No one's accusing anyone of anything—yet," Gabby couldn't resist saying, realizing that she was cutting in on Trevor's territory but unable to stop herself. Darla literally made her angry enough to see red at times. In the best of times, she didn't get along with the woman— and these were not the best of times. "But if either of you—or Trip—heard or saw anything that could help recover the missing baby, it might go a long way in smoothing out possible future—let's say *problems,*" she added euphemistically.

"You mean like a get-out-of-jail-free card," Tawny suggested.

"Something like that," Gabby agreed vaguely. If life was like a Monopoly game, she added silently—which it wasn't.

Tawny paused, as though rolling something over in her mind. Then she announced, "I saw Duke Johnson talking to someone on his phone and then he just up and left real quick-like. He looked pretty tense. Does that count?" the young woman asked.

"What time was this?" Trevor asked pointedly, deliberately not answering Tawny's question.

"About noon," the young woman estimated after another lengthy pause. "I remember because it was just before the bronco buster Mother's been hanging all over went to compete."

That was within the window of time when Avery had gone missing, Trevor thought. There was, however, just one little thing that was wrong with this scenario. "We already talked to Duke yesterday and he'd got someone to verify his alibi. When he took off like that, he told us he was going to meet up with one of the maids, Clara Peterson."

Tawny appeared completely unfazed and shrugged one indifferent shoulder. "Well, that's the only thing I noticed that looked odd. Duke had this look on his face that said he was afraid of something, and if you ask me, it had nothing to do with Clara. That woman's about as scary as a church mouse."

They'd already checked with Clara, and she had backed up Duke's claim that he was with her during the time that Faye was murdered and Avery was kidnapped. The maid had appeared a little nervous at the time, but that could easily be attributed to her reaction—along with everyone else's—to Faye's murder and to being a momentary suspect.

"We could always check her out again," Gabby suggested to Trevor once they left Darla and her daughter's quarters.

"Probably a waste of time," he speculated, dismissing the idea.

But Gabby wasn't so quick to do the same. "What does your gut tell you?" she asked. When he looked at her quizzically, she elaborated her choice of words. "You were a cop in Cheyenne. Cops are supposed to develop a kind of sixth sense about things after they've been on the job awhile."

That, he'd always felt, was based on part fact, part

myth. At least in his case. "Right now, my gut and I aren't on speaking terms," he told her.

That was because he was blocking it, she surmised. Concern about his daughter's fate was undoubtedly getting in the way of the way he normally conducted his investigations. It was understandable since he had such a vested, personal interest in the ultimate outcome of this scenario.

"Maybe you should try listening a little harder," Gabby suggested.

His normal reaction to that kind of input would have been to become defensive, but he knew that she was only trying to help.

"I suppose it wouldn't hurt to talk to Johnson again," he allowed. "Although this could just be something that your stepsister made up to throw attention and suspicion off her mother and the rest of her family."

"There is that," Gabby willingly agreed. "And just for the record," she went on to correct him, "Tawny is my *ex*-stepsister."

"Yeah, I know." He was quite clear on the family dynamics—and also on the fact that the family proper—meaning her two sisters and Gabby—had absolutely no use for the scheming woman and her like-minded adult children.

"Sorry." He saw the surprised look that came over her features. "What?"

She was genuinely surprised—and pleased. "I don't think I've ever heard you apologize before."

"Maybe I've never been wrong before," he pointed out drolly.

She laughed and shook her head. "Being wrong and knowing it would make you human—and we all know you're superhuman. What was I thinking?"

"My guess is that you weren't thinking," he dead-panned, then grew serious. "Listen, I'm going to go talk to Duke again, just to be sure."

She read her own interpretation to what was implied between the lines. "I get the feeling that I'm being 'un-invited' to the party."

"No need for both of us to go. I figure you'd want to go to the hospital and look in on your father, see how he's doing." He refrained from saying anything specific, such as whether or not the old man was still in a coma or if he was deteriorating.

A shaft of guilt swooped through her. She had got so caught up in the investigation and trying to locate Avery, as well as Faye's killer, she had almost forgotten that her father wasn't home but still in the hospital. God willing, he was conscious, but neither one of her sisters had called to say that he'd taken a turn for the better. Had it been for the worse, she knew her sisters. As long as their father wasn't on the cusp of having his health take a nosedive, they wouldn't call to tell her to come. They felt she worried too much as it was.

"Good idea," she agreed. She needed to see for herself how her father was doing and to corner a doctor about his prognosis—if that was possible. "We'll hook up again in a couple of hours," she told Trevor—then suddenly realized that she'd slipped and used a phrase that implied a great deal more than just meeting up with the man again. She struggled not to turn red. "I mean—"

He pretended not to hear her attempt at backtracking, just as he pretended not to know what the phrase she'd unintentionally used meant.

Ignoring the rather cute, endearing hue that was struggling to take over her face was a bit more difficult. Not that he liked seeing her uncomfortable, but the fact that something so negligible could embarrass her to this extent struck him as rather innocent and sweet. Women like that—he'd believed up until yesterday—didn't exist anymore.

Again he caught himself thinking that Gabby was rather unique as well as sensually attractive.

"I'll see you later," he agreed, his tone leaving no room for any further verbal exchange.

He didn't have time for the thoughts that kept trying to break in, thoughts that took Gabby's misspoken words and elaborated on them, creating images of what an actual "hookup" with her would have involved.

Hookups by definition implied casual encounters, and he was getting the very distinct feeling that there was *nothing* casual about that sort of an encounter if it occurred with Gabby. He'd initially labeled her a bleeding-heart airhead, but he was willing—at least privately—to admit that he'd misjudged her. She didn't possess a bleeding heart, she had a big heart and she was most definitely *not* an airhead. Contrarily, she had a good head on her shoulders.

She was most definitely not the type to engage in casual or whimsical sex. He rather liked that. When she played, he had the feeling it was for keeps. But, whether he liked that or not, whether he admired that or not, she deserved someone who felt the same way, who could commit to her. A man who wasn't damaged goods and didn't come with a truckload of baggage.

You've got no time for this, remember? he reminded himself. His daughter needed him and she needed him to be clear thinking.

There'd be time for the rest of it—if there *was* a rest of it, Trevor promised himself, after he brought Avery home.

Gabby's visit with her father at the hospital was relatively brief, but still fairly upsetting. He'd regained consciousness but he hadn't changed his mind concerning his future. He was just as staunchly determined not to have any treatment for his condition as he had been before he'd relapsed into a coma.

When she'd tried to reason with him and tried to get him to tell her just *why* he was refusing to seek treatment, her father had said something that she thought wasn't like him at all. He'd told her that maybe he didn't deserve to go on living and that it was time he "checked out."

Gabby tried to get him to be more specific and explain why he felt he deserved a death sentence. He refused to say any more on the subject other than it was his life to do with as he wished and that she and her sisters had absolutely no say in the matter.

Since she couldn't get him to change his mind and arguing with him was not only frustrating but emotionally taxing, Gabby left the hospital before she broke down in tears. She knew that her father had no use for tears, that he thought women who cried were emotional light weights and that tears were meant to be manipulative. He'd made it abundantly clear that he was *not* about to be manipulated by her or anyone.

Desperation had Gabby making a detour before returning to the ranch. She went to seek help from a doctor.

Specifically, she went to see Levi.

Levi was her older half brother, a product of an affair her father had had when he was still married to his first wife, Brittany. Jethro had never married Levi's mother, but that didn't change the fact that he was her half brother and she considered him family—at times, hostile family due to the way her father had treated him, but still family.

Her father certainly had got around in years past, Gabby thought as she pulled her car up before the hospital where Levi was currently doing his residency. Unlike her ne'er-do-well ex-stepsiblings, her half brother had made something of himself despite the disadvantages that faced him and the fact that his birth father felt his obligation to the child he'd sired was limited to a specified sum of money that was sent at regular intervals while Levi was an adolescent.

Levi and she, along with her sisters, knew one another and enjoyed a cordial, if somewhat distant, relationship.

Right now, however, Gabby was determined to get Levi to be something other than distant. Her father needed to receive treatment for his condition if he wanted to prolong his life. She couldn't accept that he wouldn't want to live longer. She was pinning all her hopes of getting her father to come around and act sensibly on Levi. Maybe if a physician who was also his son pointed out how foolish he was being, her father would finally listen and change his mind.

What she hadn't counted on was the fact that her father wasn't the only one who needed convincing when it came to this matter.

"You want me to do what?" Levi asked after she'd all but burst her way into the office he shared with several other doctors. His hazel eyes narrowed beneath a wayward thatch of dirty-blond hair. Was she serious?

"I want you to talk to Dad and make him get those chemo treatments. Convince him that if he doesn't, he's going to die. I don't think he *really* understands that or how serious the situation is. I *know* the disease has progressed, but at least this way, there might be some tiny bit of hope that maybe he can live longer than the doctor he'd consulted had predicted. If Dad refuses to get any treatment, then there is no hope at all."

Gabby was all but pleading with the man sitting at

the desk before her. But even though every fiber of her being was involved in this supplication, she had a feeling that her words were falling on fairly deaf ears, just the way they did when she tried to reason with her father. Levi's expression hadn't changed any since she'd begun talking. If anything, it looked as if it had actually hardened.

"You're not going to talk to him and convince him to get the treatment, are you?" she wanted to know, experiencing a sinking feeling in her stomach.

"Jethro's a big boy, Gabby," Levi reminded her mildly. He'd never been able to refer to the man with any kind of affection. The small boy within him who had desperately wanted a father had long since died. He'd made the best of life, his philosophy being it was what it was and there was no use fighting it.

He found it rather ironic that she had come to him to try to convince Jethro. After all, they had less than no relationship between them. There wasn't a single fond memory to be had that involved the blunt, driven patriarch. And he knew damn well that at this point in their lives, there never would be. "Look, Gabby, Jethro is more than capable of making up his own mind."

"Obviously, he's not," she insisted, "because if he *was* capable of making an intelligent decision, he'd be agreeing to the treatments."

"The treatments don't come with any sort of written guarantee," Levi pointed out matter-of-factly. "About the only thing that is certain is that he's going to be sick to his stomach while he's receiving treatment. It's his right to choose not to live that way."

"But it's not his right to choose *not* to live," Gabby insisted.

Levi watched her with what she felt were her father's eyes. "He might have a different opinion on that."

Frustrated, she blew out a breath. "Then it's no?" The expression on his face told her she was right—and that there was no budging him on this. "You know, whether you like it or not, Levi, you're a lot like Dad. Stubborn to the end."

"I'm nothing like him," he informed her, doing his best to bank down his annoyance.

"You go right on thinking that," she said, walking out of his office.

She was out of hearing range when he muttered a few choice words to himself. She didn't stop to ask him to repeat himself. In her present mood, that was definitely not advisable.

Hanging around Jethro Colton's hospital suite was *not* the way either of Darla's children wanted to spend their time. Neither thought matters could get worse—until their mother made her next "request" of them.

"No!" Trip told his mother before she could even finish her sentence.

"Not only no," Tawny chimed in, "but *hell no!*"

But Tawny and Trip's rather loud, disgruntled protests notwithstanding, Darla restated her demand that both of them return to Dead River for the late nanny's wake.

"I need you two to represent me at that old biddy's wake," Darla insisted, angry that she had to explain anything to her children. They should know by now that they needed to do her bidding and that was that.

"Why aren't *you* going?" Tawny, always the first to challenge her, wanted to know.

"Because I have to do something else first," Darla told her.

"So do it," Trip told her, adding his two cents to the verbal tug-of-war. "We'll wait."

"No, you'll go," Darla informed her son in no uncertain terms.

Tawny thrust out her chin, spoiling for yet another confrontation with the mother she so closely resembled. "Why?"

"Because I said so," Darla told her between tightly clenched teeth. "And if you two are partial to that allowance I've been giving you while you just sit on those no-account butts of yours, you'll do as you're told." She looked from one to the other, thinking what a disappointment to her they both were. She couldn't depend on either of them to come through for her. "Do I make myself clear?"

"Clear," Tawny muttered.

"Yeah," Trip mumbled. "Clear."

They trooped out of their former stepfather's hospital suite, clearing out the way some of the family already had.

Little by little, Jethro's room became less crowded. Everyone was headed to the wake.

Darla watched Tawny and Trip leave. Satisfied that they were on their way back to Dead River, she took herself downstairs to the hospital basement where the cafeteria was located.

There she bided her time, eating what she viewed as wretched hospital food while she waited. Waited until she was certain that everyone who'd been keeping vigil in Jethro's suite was gone. Tonight was that creature's wake, which meant that both family and staff would be there, leaving the comatose Jethro quite alone.

She didn't want anyone suddenly turning up to overhear her or, by their very presence, keep her from being able to say what she felt she needed to say.

Not that Jethro could actually hear her, but there were still things she wanted to tell him. Things that she needed to get off her chest even if the bastard couldn't hear her.

Darla smiled to herself, rather grateful that that holier-than-thou nanny had been in the wrong place at the wrong time and finally got hers.

She certainly wasn't going to be shedding any tears over *that,* Darla thought smugly.

Moving like the model she'd always thought she could have become if opportunity had been on her side, Darla entered Jethro's room and crossed over to the hospital bed where he'd been lying, unresponsive, for the past few days.

Darla always took meticulous care of her appearance, but tonight she'd taken particular care to make certain that she was even more attractive than usual.

Before entering his room again, she'd paused in the restroom to freshen up her makeup—just in case there was some minute part of Jethro that could be reached within the coma.

A tantalizing, subtle scent surrounded her like the embrace of a warm cloud.

She leaned over Jethro, lightly playing her manicured fingertips over his chest and delighting in the fact that the man hadn't regained consciousness in days.

He didn't now, either.

That he didn't respond to the way her hand languidly moved along his still torso told her he was still in the grips of the coma.

A wide smile touched her blazing red lips as she whispered into his ear, "Looks like I get my wish, you old bastard. Christmas comes early this year. You're really dying. And I must say, it couldn't be happening to a more deserving man."

She straightened up, still looking at him.

"I am surprised, though, that you're not grasping at every straw, trying to bribe and claw your way back to good health like the pathetic creature you are. Refraining just isn't like you. But it goes without saying that I *am* very pleased that you're refusing treatment. The faster you go, the faster I get my money. And believe me, I fully intend to get what's mine." She patted her chest for emphasis. "Because I've *earned* it.

"Every time you made love to me, every time I had to endure the sight of those spindly little legs of yours

and that thin, pathetic naked body, I'd placate myself
by fantasizing about your death, about spreading out
my share of the money all over your dead body." She
smirked with glee.

"I just can't *wait* to see you in the ground. The very
thought of it makes me feel all hot and excited with
anticipation."

She glanced at her watch and then the Cheshire-
cat grin returned. "Well, what do you know, the stores
aren't closing for another hour. I think I'll go shopping
for my 'mourning dress.' Something bright and color-
ful seems appropriate, don't you think? It'll be perfect
for when I dance on your grave."

She leaned in close to his ear one final time and
whispered, "Nobody's going to miss you, you wasted
piece of flesh. Least of all, me."

With a laugh that lingered, along with her scent,
long after she left her ex-husband's hospital suite, Darla
walked out of the room.

He'd heard her.

Heard every mean-spirited word Darla had uttered.

Locked in the grasp of a dusky netherworld that for-
bade and restrained any sort of movement, he'd still
been able to hear her.

Jethro had always thought that it would end this way.
There were many who thought he deserved an ignoble
ending and he was among them. Never a particularly
good man, he'd only grown less so as the years went by.

The sins he was guilty of were many.

At times, he would have been hard-pressed to say which of those sins was the most grievous. The women he'd bedded and abandoned?

The children he'd fathered and turned his back on?

The son he had lost?

His connection to organized crime, which had stretched out over not years but decades?

There were other sins, a score or so more, sins he couldn't even recall, but that had blackened his already-black soul.

Yes, he had this coming; there was no doubt about that.

The only thing that truly irked him about his departing this world was that his pending demise gladdened the heart of the harpy who had just been hovering over him. But then, she would get hers in the end. The money she was expecting to receive would never materialize. It would vanish like so much dust in the wind—just as he was destined to do.

Despite the reckless life he'd led, he'd always known that in the end there would be justice—dispensed by a judge who presided over them all.

A judge to whom there was no appeal because he had witnessed it all and meted out punishment that fit the crime or, as in his case, the crimes.

He wasn't ready to die—who ever was?—but he accepted it as his fate and refused to prolong the agony, neither his own, nor his family's, by seeking out treatment that came with no guarantees and put forth no promises.

He deserved what was coming to him and he would take it like a man.

There was a first time for everything.

Chapter 13

The moment the medical examiner completed his autopsy and released Faye's body, Dylan immediately had his mother's remains transported to the town's only funeral home. Though it was hard for him, he carefully went through his mother's things and chose her favorite dress so that she could be buried in it.

Rather than having the funeral home hold a wake for his mother that extended over three days, Dylan requested that the wake be only for one evening. Contacting the minister of the church Faye had attended on occasion, he made arrangements for her funeral to be held the next morning. She was his mother, and even in death, he was protective of her. He wanted her away from prying, curious eyes as soon as respectfully possible.

"Guess I'm not as grown up as I thought, Ma," Dylan Frick whispered to the woman within the coffin. His throat threatened to close up on him.

He'd deliberately hung back, waiting in the rear of the funeral home's dimly lit viewing room for everyone who wanted to pay their last respects to come, say their piece or their fragmented prayers and then leave.

She was being buried tomorrow morning.

He wanted to spend these last few moments alone with her.

Or what there was of his mother now that she was dead.

He'd thought that he could hold it together. That though he felt bereft at her abrupt, violent and utterly untimely passing, he could successfully deal with the emptiness that he was attempting to ignore, the emptiness that was eating away at him, giving no indication that it could be vanquished anytime within the foreseeable future.

He'd thought—until now—that he was strong enough not to allow tears to gather in his eyes. Certainly strong enough not to allow them to fall.

But apparently it seemed that he had no control over that, no matter how much he tried. Hence his whispered comment about his not being grown up enough.

But, he'd come to learn, within each grown man was a child aching to be comforted. A child who realized that he never would be comforted again.

"I should have taken the time to tell you how much

you meant to me, how good a mother I thought you were," he murmured to the still face, berating himself.

Dylan thought of the parade of wives and mistresses that Jethro Colton had gone through, not to mention the one who still lived on the premises like some unexorcised evil spirit.

"God knows there were enough bad ones around us for me to be able to see the difference, to realize how very special you are—were," he corrected himself, hating the fact that he had to.

Dylan sighed and it came out sounding more like a shudder.

Maybe it was a little bit of both.

"But I always thought there'd be more time, that I could say what I knew I should say to you later. I was supposed to have later," he said in almost an accusing tone, even though he knew it wasn't her fault. That if there *was* a fault, it was his.

"It wasn't supposed to be over yet." The tears were back, and this time, he didn't even bother trying to hold them back. "You were supposed to be around so I could give you those grandkids I knew you wanted. Now those kids, if I ever have them, will never get to know you, will never be able to brag to other kids that they've got the best grandmother in the state of Montana."

Just then, his voice cracked. Filled with emotion, he couldn't speak. All he could do was feel as if he'd just been robbed. Robbed of a mother, robbed of the years he'd thought they still had.

"I'll get him, Ma. Whoever did this to you, I swear

I'll get him and I'll make him pay for it. He can't get away with it, can't get away with just cutting you down like that."

Dylan pressed his lips together, really afraid that at any second, he was going to break down.

Because of the rug, he didn't hear the footsteps approaching until the person was directly behind him.

And then next to him.

"She looks like she's sleeping, doesn't she?" Mathilda Perkins asked, coming up behind him.

His back to the woman, Dylan quickly dried the tearstains on his face with the back of his hand. "No, ma'am," he replied stoically. "She doesn't. Ma used to toss and turn, like something was after her when she slept."

He remembered how that used to worry him when he was a little boy. That he used to think she entered another world when she slept and that someday, she just wouldn't come back. Years later, when he shared that with her, she just laughed and said she slept fitfully because, as the head nanny on the ranch, she always had a great deal on her mind.

"She never looked this peaceful," he told the other woman.

His hat in his hand as he stood before her casket, Dylan absently ran the edge of the brim through his fingers. His eyes narrowed ever so slightly as he studied the housekeeper.

"I thought you came by earlier," he said to the woman.

"I did." She wondered how he knew that, since when

she was here, she hadn't seen him. "But I wanted to talk to you and I thought I'd eventually find you here, so I came back."

"Talk to me?" he repeated. Other than words of condolences, the woman had hardly spared ten words on him in the past twenty years. "About what?"

"About all this." Mathilda gestured about the funeral parlor. "About the funeral."

He had no idea where this was going or what the woman was trying to say. There was something about Mathilda Perkins that made him uneasy, although for the life of him, he couldn't have said what—or if it was actually because he felt so ripped up inside.

"What about the funeral?" he asked her.

Mathilda paused, as if she were searching for just the right words to use. After several beats, she continued.

"Well, all this costs money, as you well know, the high cost of dying and all that," the woman elaborated, referring to an old cliché, "and I know that since you're still struggling to establish yourself, money is undoubtedly more than a little tight."

Mathilda stopped and then started again, hoping to sound more coherent this time around.

"So I wanted to tell you that I'd like to help pay for the casket and the service." She offered him a compassionate smile, as if responding to some mental cue card that was suddenly being held up. "Your mother was my friend and this is the least I can do for her."

Did the woman really think he was poor or was

something else at work here? "No disrespect intended, Ms. Perkins, but I can pay for Ma's funeral."

"Please—" Mathilda lightly placed her hand on his wrist, silently supplicating Dylan. "I feel as if I owe it to her," the housekeeper insisted.

"I feel the same way, Ms. Perkins," Dylan told her, "and blood comes first."

Mathilda looked at him for a long moment. He didn't know, she realized. Faye obviously had never told him, taking her secret to the grave.

"Yes," she murmured. "Blood comes first," she agreed. And then she squeezed his hand quickly. "All right, I won't press this. But if you ever need anything, or I can help you in some small way, you know where you can find me."

With that, she retreated, leaving him alone with his mother again.

Dylan waited until the housekeeper's footsteps echoed down the corridor, away from the viewing room where his mother was laid out.

He shook his head, thinking of the housekeeper and the rather eerie feeling she'd created in her own wake. "I always thought you had better taste in friends, Ma."

Moving to the first row of chairs before the casket, Dylan picked a seat and sat down. He stayed there, watching over his mother's casket and mentally reviewing his memories for a very long time.

Wishing with all his heart that he'd had just a little more time with his mother before her end had come.

But even a world of time wouldn't have been enough. All it would have done, Dylan thought, was make him want even more.

There was no reason for Gabby to stop by the hospital. Her father continued to be comatose and her sisters had promised to call her if there was the slightest change in his condition.

Amanda and Catherine were taking turns staying at his bedside, but the urgency of keeping vigil was lessening as it appeared that their father was not about to suddenly come out of his coma. Besides, Gabby knew for a fact that all the doctors had been notified to immediately call the family should there be no one at Jethro's bedside when and if he *did* emerge from his coma, the way he'd done once before.

Gabby supposed that in the absolute sense, she'd be of more use to Trevor than coming here, because the more people actively looking for his daughter, the better the chances were of finding the three-month-old. But for the sake of her conscience, she'd told Trevor that she wanted to swing by the hospital for a few minutes to see for herself how her father was doing.

She got no argument from Trevor, who still maintained that he really didn't *need* her help, despite the fact that he seemed to welcome it—or, more accurately, he wasn't rejecting her help with nearly as much verve as he had been.

Victories, Gabby thought as the hospital elevator

stopped on her father's floor and she got out, came in all sorts of various shapes and sizes.

Because of the late hour, the hospital corridors were eerily empty. There was less of a staff on duty after nine in the evening. The lights had been dimmed in order to enable the patients along that floor to fall asleep more easily.

Her father's room was amid the suites reserved for the most affluent of patients, the ones who preferred their rooms to resemble hotel suites with all the amenities that went along with that sort of a high price tag.

Wealth, Gabby thought, *has its privileges.* Although it couldn't buy you health at any price, it could most certainly buy you comfort. Not that comfort meant all that much to her father in his present state.

Opening the door to her father's suite, Gabby silently slipped in. She knew it was Catherine's turn to take the shift, and since her sister wasn't in the room, Gabby assumed that she had probably gone to get herself some coffee.

Just as well, Gabby thought. She wanted to have her father to herself for the few minutes that she had to spare before going back to the ranch.

Gabby crossed to her father's bedside. He looked, for all the world, as if he were just in a deep sleep—except for the tubes and monitors that formed a semicircle around him, keeping track of his vital signs and his breathing and making certain that his fluid needs were met.

Very gently, Gabby took his hand in hers and laced

her fingers with his. It still felt like such a powerful hand, but perhaps, on closer look, it was just a tad less so.

Gabby sighed.

"Still playing possum, I see. Not that I can blame you, considering how many bad feelings you touched off, saying you wouldn't ransom Trevor's daughter. That's not how you're supposed to respond to a situation like that, Dad," she reminded him reprovingly. "Trevor's one of your people. You're supposed to help your people, or didn't anyone ever teach you that?" she asked.

"No, I guess not," she decided a moment later. "But then, things like that shouldn't have to be taught—you should just instinctively know them." She pressed her lips together as she looked at the ashen-faced man in the hospital bed. There was a time when she'd thought of him as being such an indestructible giant. She'd been certain back then that nothing could ever harm him. But now she knew better.

And he wasn't her hero anymore, the way he had been when she was a child.

"I love you, Dad. There are times—like now—when I don't much like you, but I do love you. I always will, you know. All the same, I sure wish you hadn't behaved so shamefully about ransoming Trevor's baby. Avery was kidnapped because they thought she was your granddaughter, so, you see, you do have sort of a responsibility to do what you can to bring her back."

Gabby squared her shoulders, wondering if she were crazy, or at the very least, wasting her breath talking to a comatose person as if he could hear every word. But saying it made her feel better, not deceitful.

"I just want you to know that if we do get a ransom note, I intend to use my trust-fund money. I know you have the final say in this, but right now, you can't say anything, so I'm going ahead as if you'd given your permission. Being ornery, knowing what I'm about to do will probably make you come out of your coma, but I figure either way, I win. And if this does make you come out of your coma and you still veto giving any money to bring that baby home, I'll find another way to raise the money. Coltons always live up to their responsibilities—you taught me that. And bringing Avery home safely is *my* responsibility."

Gabby stood over her father for another long moment, a jumble of words crowding her head, myriad emotions crowding her heart. But there wasn't enough time to say and act on everything she was feeling right now.

"I know you, old man," she whispered in his ear so that no one could overhear her just in case her sister suddenly returned. Her throat felt thick with tears she couldn't take the time to shed right how. Tears that filled her soul. "You're too cantankerous to die. You'll be back. I know you'll be back. Just don't make us wait too long."

Gabby pressed a kiss to her father's forehead. She thought she felt him stir just the slightest bit, but when she drew back to look, he appeared to be just as he had been when she'd walked in.

Just my imagination, she told herself. Wishful thinking.

The door to the suite opened just then and Catherine walked in, a half-consumed container of coffee in her hand. Obviously not expecting anyone to be in the room, her sister looked surprised to see her.

"Gabby, what are you doing here?" she asked. Her eyes widened in the next moment. "Did they find Avery?"

Gabby shook her head. "Not yet. I just wanted to stop by and see how Dad was doing."

It wasn't as if the hospital was a quick hop, skip and a jump away from the house. It took a while to get here. Catherine shook her head. "I promised to call if there was any change," she reminded Gabby.

"I know, I know," Gabby said, in no mood to be on the receiving end of even the slightest lecture. "I guess I just wanted to see the old man myself."

"Still looks the same," Catherine assured her, settling into the chair that was facing the bed. "Mean," she concluded, then added, "Notice that he doesn't look any friendlier unconscious than he does when he's wide-awake?"

There was no arguing that. "I notice."

Gabby gathered herself together. She'd said what she'd come to say. That she loved him, no matter how he behaved, but that she was also planning to do what needed to be done, even if it was going against the last thing he'd said were his wishes. Brushing a kiss to the grizzled cheek, she stepped away from the bed and turned to her sister. "I'll see you soon," she told Catherine by way of a parting.

Catherine nodded. "One way or another," her sister murmured.

That was, Gabby knew, Catherine's way of dealing with the situation: thinking herself past it.

"One way or another," Gabby echoed, leaving.

By the time the door to her father's hospital suite closed behind her, Gabby was mentally already back with Trevor, fully entrenched in the ongoing search for Avery.

Chapter 14

Four days of intensive questioning and they were no further along in tracking down Faye's killer or the person/persons responsible for kidnapping Avery than they'd been by the end of the first day. Trevor had secretly hoped that both the questions would have been resolved by the time they buried Faye. But the slain nanny's funeral had come and gone and still the questions remained.

Who had done this and why? And where was Avery?

The situation was taking a definite toll on Trevor. Drained, frustrated and verging on desperate, he'd returned to the wing of the mansion he occupied. Because she was concerned about him, Gabby had insisted on coming with him to make sure he went home rather than going off somewhere half-cocked.

He'd been silent on the ride back to the ranch, but

she was getting used to that, even though she still didn't like it.

And then, as he unlocked his door and walked in, he broke his self-imposed silence by saying, "The first twenty-four hours after a kidnapping are crucial. After that, chances of finding the victim alive are drastically reduced with every passing hour. And we've passed a lot of hours."

He found that he had to struggle not to punch his fist through a wall. The only thing stopping him was that he knew it wouldn't help relieve his tension and, most likely, might wreak havoc on his knuckles.

Gabby felt for him more than she could hope to express. She eased the door closed behind them. She really didn't want to leave him alone just yet. Not with black thoughts as his only companions. "Trevor, you can't give up hope."

"Don't give me platitudes," he snapped at her angrily. "I know what I know. I was a cop, dealing with all the ugliness the world can throw at you while you—you were living in fantasyland," he jeered. "Nobody's called demanding a ransom. That means one of two things. Either Avery was kidnapped by someone who wanted a kid of their own, or they realized they snatched the wrong kid and they're not going to get a plug nickel for her." His jaw had hardened, but she saw that there was untapped emotion in his eyes. She realized that he was afraid. Not for himself, but for the infant he'd initially rejected. He was being twice as hard on himself for that. "They killed someone in the process, so they're not just gonna give her back. And we keep hitting dead ends. She's gone," he pronounced, his voice hollow and edgy.

But Gabby shook her head. For the first time, he saw her eyes flash with anger. It seemed to change her countenance entirely. "No, I'm not going to accept that."

"Like it changes anything if you do or not," he retorted. What she thought, what she said, didn't change the situation even a fraction of an iota—no matter how much either one of them wished that it did.

Gabby fired back the names of two famous abducted girls, both of whom had made headlines in their time. One had gone missing for months; the other had literally been missing for years in her time.

"Everybody gave up on *ever* finding them, and they both turned up alive. The first one was rescued *years* after she was abducted on her way to school, the second one just under a year from the time she was snatched out of her own bed with her terrified younger sister actually looking on."

Gabby thought of another example to cite as she was talking. "And there was that boy who'd only managed to escape when he decided to save another little boy who'd been taken from his home the same way he had. That was years after he was taken."

Trevor had turned away from her, but she deliberately got into his face as she insisted, "Not all kidnapped victims turn up dead, Trevor."

Still, the statistics were against them. "A lot of them do."

"Avery *won't*," Gabby insisted firmly. "We're going

to find her—and we won't give up until we do," she told him with conviction.

He laughed shortly, even though, inside, he wanted desperately to be convinced. "And just what makes you so sure?"

She never wavered under his intense scrutiny. "I just am. I can feel it inside," she said, her hand pressing on her abdomen. "It's a gut feeling. Don't cops rely on gut feelings a lot?" she said.

She was simplifying things way too much, he couldn't help thinking. Nothing was that black-and-white anymore. "They've got forensics now."

He was trying to get her to back off, she thought—and she wasn't about to let him. "Gut feelings have been around a lot longer than forensics," Gabby pointed out, stubbornly clinging to her argument and her insistence that he remain positive.

Trevor dragged his hand through his hair, feeling so frustrated he couldn't even contemplate his next move, couldn't even put what he was feeling into words.

Outside his window, the world had gone dark. As dark as any shred of hope he had initially been harboring at the outset.

And yet there she was, wanting to rally him. He understood what she was trying to do and he appreciated it, even though he wasn't receptive toward it. "You really believe what you're saying?" he asked.

"Yes, I really believe what I'm saying," she answered with emphasis.

Gabby meant no harm, he told himself. She was

Pollyanna, trying to give him a sliver of hope. He nodded, accepting her words for what they were: desperate cries into the merciless wind. "I didn't mean to bite off your head just now."

She waved away his apology, secretly stunned to hear another one from him. "That's okay. I'm getting used to it. If you didn't bite my head off just then, I would have figured you weren't paying attention to what I was saying." She put her hand on his shoulder, silently offering her comfort and support, wishing there was a way to infuse that into him. "We *will* find her, Trevor," she told him quietly for what felt like the umpteenth time. "We will."

The words, coupled with the gentle contact, got to him. They found the chink in the battered armor he surrounded himself with and got through.

Trevor took the hand she'd placed on his shoulder and rather than remove it, or toss it off the way she expected him to, he completely surprised her when he turned her hand palm side up and pressed a kiss into it.

It wasn't meant to be a sensual kiss. It was the kiss of a man who was grateful, a man who was struggling and doing his best not to cave in and crumple under the weight of things he feared were going to come to pass.

"She's so little," he murmured helplessly.

Gabby immediately gravitated toward the silver lining. "The good thing is that she's too young to have any memory of this—once it's behind her," she emphasized.

"*If* we find her," Trevor qualified. He couldn't remember *ever* feeling as helpless as he did right at this

minute. And he didn't do "helpless" well. It made him
edgy and uptight. That wasn't exactly a revelation, but
to feel it was utterly disconcerting, to say the least.

But he was feeling so much more than just discon-
certed. *This* was literally a life-and-death scenario he
was contemplating and doing so was almost too much
for him.

"*When* we find her, Trevor," Gabby stressed, then, in
case she was actually wearing him down, she repeated,
"*When* we find her."

Trevor looked into her eyes for a very long moment.
She wasn't the airheaded little optimist anymore. Instead, he saw Gabby as a woman of strength, of determination. A woman who could keep her head on straight
while everyone else was running around, losing theirs.

"Your horses never do come into the stable, do they?"
he said, referring to a comment he'd made in anger the
day his daughter had been taken.

"Only to refuel," Gabby replied, offering him the
brightest smile she could. And even as she did, she
could feel herself being drawn to him, thinking of how
hard his physique felt beneath her hand.

Feeling a host of emotions that had nothing to do
with the immediate situation.

She shouldn't be feeling this, Gabby silently up-
braided herself. The man was dealing with the most
horrible situation that could confront any parent. He
had pressure coming at him from all sides. This was *no*
time to think of him as anything but a distraught father
facing a parent's worst nightmare.

And yet, when he'd kissed her hand like that, all sorts of feelings—urgent, insistent feelings—had instantly risen to the surface, making her react to him on a very basic, intense level.

Making her hunger for a reenactment of that kiss they'd shared.

Making her want that and more.

So very much more.

She knew she had to leave before the last thin bands of her restraint broke. Her lips were all but parched as she said, "I'd better go and let you get some rest."

"I'm not going to rest," Trevor told her, then added, "You know that."

"But you should," she insisted. "You're not a machine—you're still human."

It would have been better if he *was* a machine. Then he would be able to focus clearly, without being distracted. "I'm too tense," he told her honestly.

"Then find a way to release that," she advised. "Or you'll be a zombie by tomorrow morning and no good to anyone, least of all yourself or Avery."

"Avery," he repeated. His voice, choked with emotion, said everything there was to be said about his feelings for his infant daughter. He wished he could think the way Gabby did. "How does someone tap into that endless optimism of yours?"

Her smile was unreadable, but sweet nonetheless. "I wish I could say it's transferable, that I could just touch your cheek or your hand, and you'd feel what I feel—but it doesn't work that way," she concluded sadly.

He moved in closer then, and she saw the desperation in his eyes. Desperation and something more, something she discovered she couldn't read, couldn't identify. All she knew was that she wanted to comfort him, to make him shed that oppressive cloak of pessimism he had draped around his shoulders and his very soul.

Without thinking it through, she reacted on a basic gut level.

She kissed him.

The gentle kiss was meant to comfort him, to rally him and make him able to entertain the slightest shred of hope. It was *not* intended to open any floodgates— but it did.

For him.

For her.

And, like a stick of dynamite with a very short fuse, something went off within each of them, detonating simultaneously.

Rather than a calming effect, the kiss, gentle in nature though it was, had the exact opposite effect.

One kiss gave birth to another, and another.

And another.

Each one more powerful, more all-encompassing than the last.

Latent, trapped passion was released within each of them with such a high flare, as if what was inside had been waiting all this time for the right set of circumstances, the right moment and the right catalyst to ignite it.

Rather than pull back, embarrassed and murmuring

apologies or excuses, Gabby was drawn to him as the heat of the moment gave way to a frenzy of desire and movement encased in passion.

Thoughts, actions, they all became a blur, all occurring almost out of the reach of consciousness. The only thing that seemed to dominate her was need. The need to comfort and perhaps to be comforted. The very real need to be needed.

If he were asked to re-create the scene that was unfolding at this very moment, re-create it just seconds after the fact, Trevor wouldn't have been able to. His detail-oriented mind had gone completely missing in action.

All he knew was that he wanted her, needed what she had to offer.

Needed her.

What he *was* aware of was the taste of her, the smell of her, the very feel of her. It all seemed to swirl around him, intensifying the urgency he felt, the urgency to take her, to lose himself in her and to have that very action smother all outside thoughts and concerns. He wanted to have, to feel, what she felt. He wanted her hope and maybe, just maybe, by having her, by finally allowing himself to react to her the way a man reacted to a desirable woman, he could be transformed.

He could somehow *absorb* that positive aura she radiated. And, for a little while, perhaps he'd even be whole.

A hundred and one sensations scrambled through her at the same time, and Gabby was desperate to grab on to them, to savor each one, but that would have involved choosing between them, choosing which to luxuriate in first—and she wasn't capable of that. Greedy for the first time in her life, she wanted them all.

He was creating mini eruptions within her just by running his hands along her body, just by bringing his mouth down on her heated skin.

She had no clear memory of where her clothes went or how they'd actually left her body. Didn't remember if she was the one who actually shed them one by one, or if Trevor had taken them off her.

She vaguely remembered grabbing on to his shirt and pulling it from his hard, sculpted torso.

But after that, the only thing that she was fairly clear on was the sweeping parade of climaxes, great and small, that danced through her as this taciturn cowboy created magic all along her body, weaving the magic both inside and out.

She was aware of twisting against him, aware of wanting him so badly she thought she was going to explode, more than once, all by herself, if he didn't finally take her.

As he did come closer, his body covering hers, she instinctively wrapped her legs around him to hold him prisoner and prevent any further delays if he was entertaining the idea of prolonging this exquisite agony that was already stretching out to infinity, jarring her teeth.

Jarring her body.

She was making him crazy.

Pressing her body into his, arching against him like

that, weaving her legs around him like some sort of agile nymph, she was taking him prisoner. He wasn't his own master anymore.

Offering herself to him over and over again the way she was, Trevor found he had nowhere to retreat to. Nowhere to go in order to regroup and try to summon back the black-and-white common sense that had ruled his life for so long.

She was the princess and he was the help. He had nothing to offer her and absolutely no right to be doing what he was doing.

No right wanting her the way he did.

But damn, she was making it far too hard for him to be able to just pick up and walk away. Hell, he didn't even know *if* he could actually walk. She'd made him not just weak in the knees, but completely weak all over.

All except for his desire, which was so incredibly intense, so incredibly strong, that before he knew it, it commandeered center stage.

And then he found himself taking her.

Unable to resist her any longer, unable to resist his own desire any longer, Trevor uttered a groan of surrender as he moved into her. Her legs tightened even harder around him. He honestly hadn't thought that it was physically possible.

And yet it was.

The movement began automatically, the symphony of their souls utterly in sync, each thrust begetting another and another until, breathless, overwhelmed, they rose to the top of the peak as one, joined in body as they were joined in spirit.

And then they leaped off the summit, still joined together in purpose, still as one.

Gradually, he became aware of the heavy, labored breathing. He thought it was hers, until he realized that the sounds were coming from him.

Very slowly, Trevor descended to earth, relinquishing his hold on—his place in—paradise.

His surroundings came into focus, as did his memory.

They were in his bed, the blanket and sheets beneath her tangled and all but stripped off the bed from the sheer frenzy of their lovemaking.

As he fell back onto his bed he realized that his skin came in contact with his mattress, not his sheets. Well, *that* had never happened before, but then making love had never been a high priority with him before, either. It happened when it happened, but it had never been a driving force in his life.

He couldn't truthfully say that anymore.

If he could have, he would have just vanished from the scene, found a way to disappear without the need to exchange any dialogue or even be seen.

But he couldn't just get up and leave now. For one thing, this was *his* bedroom, not hers. For another, if he left in silence, he wouldn't have been able to return; it would just be too awkward.

Besides, he'd made a connection with her—almost against his will, but he'd made it. That wasn't some-

thing he could turn his back on, even if he wanted to—
which he didn't.

Now all he needed was a way to start some sort of
verbal exchange between them.

His mind went blank.

The silence grew louder until it was almost deafen-
ing in nature.

The inside of his mouth grew drier.

Chapter 15

The silence within Trevor's bedroom completely engulfed her—or so it seemed.

Had it gone *that* badly for him? Either way, why wasn't he saying *something?*

Finally, she couldn't take it anymore.

"I know you're a man of few words," Gabby began, picking her own words carefully, "but this is setting a record, even for you. Please say something."

It wasn't exactly an order or a plea, but the silence, now that the euphoria had abated, was *really* getting to her—big-time—and making her exceedingly uncomfortable.

She didn't regret what had happened—how could she? The experience—at least for her—was the most incredible one of her limited twenty-four years. She'd never felt anything so intense, so moving in her life. It was as close to an out-of-body experience as she'd ever had or probably *would* ever have.

Her entire body, when it had finally floated back to earth, had felt as if it were smiling. That wasn't something to regret. On the contrary, she wanted to repeat this glorious experience—and soon.

But not if the whole interlude had rendered him close to catatonic.

"You haven't been struck speechless, have you?" Gabby prodded. "Say *something*," she said again, this time with a great deal more emphasis.

Trevor took a breath, shifting his body so that it turned into hers. He shifted his eyes as well. Finally, he murmured a very simple, unadorned phrase. "Didn't see that coming."

Gabby propped herself up not just on her elbow but pushed herself up with her hand so that she gained some height over his resting torso. She gazed down into his face.

"Really?" she asked, not knowing whether to be amused or stunned that he had been caught so unaware by what had just happened. "You had no clue?"

She really found that difficult to believe, especially since she'd had an inkling that this was on the horizon for a while now. Something in her bones had whispered to her that they'd be together like this sometime in the future, maybe even the near future.

And here they were.

A sheepish smile curved the corners of Trevor's

mouth. He supposed that he did sound pretty clueless at that. For once, he took no offense at the less-than-flattering image she was verbally painting.

"Guess I was just too busy focusing on other things to realize what was going on right in front of my eyes," he admitted.

She was surprised that he took her words and just accepted them. The man wasn't all that unreasonable at that.

"I guess so," she agreed. She laid her head on his chest, her red hair fanning out across the firm, wide expanse.

Without thinking, he ran his fingers along the silky waves. His breathing slowly returned to something that resembled normal, even though his heart insisted on beating erratically.

"Now what?"

Trevor asked the question so quietly, for a moment, she thought she'd just imagined it. But then she became aware that he appeared to be waiting for some sort of a response from her.

"Now we get back to looking for Avery," she told him, her breath along his skin making the muscles beneath it quiver, then tighten.

He wasn't referring to that when he'd asked "now what?" Granted, finding Avery was uppermost in his mind. However, what had just happened here had temporarily overshadowed it. The past hour wasn't just a one-night stand to him. He'd had one-night stands, had a number of them to look back on, and they were merely vague, isolated incidents that only became more so with the passage of time. They'd happened, he'd enjoyed them while they were occurring and then they were behind him, meriting not even so much as a few minutes' worth of reflection.

This, in comparison, had been different.

It was the difference between grabbing a nondescript sandwich and having a three-course meal at a five-star restaurant that lingered not just on his taste buds, but in his memory as well.

Was she saying that this was just a one-night stand as far as she was concerned? He didn't know how he felt about that.

Ordinarily, he might have welcomed that sort of a reaction from her—especially if he'd felt this way. Other than Avery's mother, he'd never had entanglements with the women he'd slept with. After the event, he'd always gone his separate way, as had they.

But this was different.

He wasn't sure he liked Gabby behaving as if there was no strong, compelling reaction on her part, the way there had been on his.

"I wasn't talking about Avery," Trevor began to explain slowly.

His eyes were on hers.

A trap.

It was a trap, she thought.

He was setting her up, daring her to say what was *really* on her mind—and once she did, once she let him know that the earth *had* moved for her, he'd have an excuse to never allow anything of this nature to happen again. Because Trevor Garth wasn't a man who could be tied down to one woman, one family. She knew that and she didn't want to tie him down. She just wanted to be the one he turned to whenever the need for a kindred soul hit him.

Gabby was aware that feeling this way made it sound as if she were settling, but some things, unlike some sort of a movie rental, couldn't be achieved quickly and on demand. Some things, such as a worthwhile relationship with a man like Trevor, took time to cultivate. And, luckily for her, she just happened to be a patient soul.

"But we should be," she told him, then because he appeared somewhat confused, she realized that he'd probably lost the thread of the conversation as he was trying to figure her out. "We *should* be talking about Avery," she further elaborated.

Gathering the sheet to her as best she could to cover up her nakedness, Gabby sat up, her eyes riveted to his face despite the fact that there were a few far more enticing sections of his anatomy to draw and captivate her attention.

"There's got to be something we've missed," she insisted.

They'd spent close to a week talking to everyone on the ranch and every friend of every staff member just to confirm the alibis they'd been given and then they'd confirmed the confirmations.

Right about now it felt as if they were spinning worn tires in the mud: lots of noise, no traction.

Trevor sat up as well, oblivious for the need of any sort of cover for his body. He dragged his hand through his hair, as if that could somehow unearth a theretofore untapped avenue to follow, leading to a discovery that hadn't been made yet.

Coming up empty, he sighed. "I agree with you," he told her. "But for the life of me, I don't know what it could be, other than…" His voice trailed off as he contemplated the daunting recourse left to them.

"Other than what?" Gabby prodded. Had he thought of something they hadn't tried?

"Other than the possibility that someone was lying to us, which means that we'll have to question everyone in the house a second time and check their alibis again to see if they still check out."

He expected Gabby to groan loudly and then perhaps to opt out of the overwhelming task of starting at the beginning again. What he didn't expect was to have her agree with him.

"Someone obviously was," Gabby told him. "So, unless one of us has suddenly developed the art of mind reading, or clairvoyance, that's exactly what we're going to have to do. Question everyone all over again. Who knows," she speculated, "maybe someone will slip up, forget what they said the first time around and we'll finally have them—and Avery."

With effort, Gabby continued to look only into Trevor's face, although it wasn't easy. "Right now, it's our only recourse."

He nodded. Glancing through the window, he saw

that it was still pitch-black and estimated that they were approaching midnight. "Okay, I'll get started first thing in the morning."

Didn't he realize yet that after almost a whole week at this, she was in this for the long haul?

"*We'll* get started first thing in the morning," she corrected.

It amazed him how much the way he regarded Gabby had changed in the course of a few days. He'd started out blaming her for what had happened to his daughter and now he was almost depending on her for help in locating the infant.

Depending on her and—although he would never admit this to her—drawing comfort from her very presence.

"In the meantime," he continued, "that still leaves us tonight to deal with." His eyes swept over her face. He'd never realized how delicate her face looked yet how very determined it seemed at the same time. "Any ideas?" he asked her.

She gave up staring exclusively at his face and allowed her eyes to dip down to at least take in his upper physique.

"Oh, I've got *lots* of ideas," Gabby assured him.

The smile on his face told her they were on the same page.

The following morning, Gabby was already up and dressed when he opened his eyes.

"Going somewhere?" he asked, stretching his frame as he allowed himself to come to by degrees.

Rather than beat around the bush and attempt to be coy, Gabby was completely honest with him. "I'm sneaking out of here before someone comes knocking on your door and discovers that your reputation has been compromised, Mr. Head of Security."

"I don't know about *compromised*. More than likely, they'd applaud me for my good taste," he cracked. Awake now, he swung his legs out of his bed and stood up.

Gabby averted her eyes as she turned her head. But even so, a pink hue instantly began recoloring her cheeks. Again, he caught himself thinking that he hadn't thought women could blush anymore. That she could was something he found to be rather endearing.

His broad smile, though, evaporated the next moment when there was a knock on his door.

Talk about foreshadowing...

Gabby barely had time to suck in her breath, looking around the room to see if there was somewhere for her to hide.

The next moment, she decided that she was, after all, a grown woman and entitled to make her own choices. The only one who would have made her want to disappear from the room without a trace was her father, and he was still in the hospital, unable, for the moment, to heap insults on her head.

When she turned toward Trevor to ask if he wanted her to answer the door, she saw that he was already dressed, his jeans covering his muscular lower torso and the shirt he'd had on last night back in place this morning. The man was fast, she thought in admiration.

The only hint that they were doing something other than just talking in his room was that he was barefoot.

But then, this was, after all, his room. She was the foreign element, the one who didn't belong in the room.

The knock on the door was timid and gave the impression that if the door wasn't immediately opened, whoever was standing on the other side would just go away.

He couldn't have that, Trevor thought. Not knowing who it was would keep him up for weeks.

When he pulled the door open, neither he nor Gabby was prepared to see the young woman who was standing at his threshold.

Gabby found her voice first.

"Clara?" Gabby asked, curious and stunned at the same time. Stepping discreetly into the hallway, she looked up and down both corridors, but there was no one else around. "What are you doing here?" she asked, stepping back inside the bedroom.

The young maid didn't answer immediately. Instead, she knotted and unknotted her fingers, looking exceptionally flustered and uncomfortable.

"I need to talk to Mr. Trevor," she finally explained nervously. Consumed with why she was here, Clara didn't appear to think that it was the slightest bit strange to find her employer's youngest daughter inside of the head of security's room. "I went to your office, but you weren't there yet," she told him nervously.

"No, I wasn't," Trevor agreed, doing his best not to laugh, even as it occurred to him that it was an odd reaction for him in the first place. But then, having spent the night with Gabby had made him feel almost light-headed. Certainly light-spirited. It was altogether a new experience for him.

Pulling himself together, he forced himself to focus on the pale young woman who'd sought him out. "Why are you looking for me?"

Clara looked close to tears. "Because I don't want to go to hell."

"All right," he said, stretching out the words as he exchanged glances with Gabby. "And why would you be going to hell?"

It took Clara a few minutes to form an answer, and when she did, she blurted out the words. "For lying to you."

Instantly, the humor of the moment and everything that had come before faded into the background. This was serious.

"And what is it that you lied to me about?" he asked.

It was obvious that the shift in his tone frightened the maid to the point of near incoherence. Her expression was that of a deer caught in not one but two sets of headlights.

"You have to understand, I was just trying to protect him because he was afraid that if you found out what he was doing, you'd have him fired."

Gabby could see Trevor's agitation growing. She could also see that Clara was terrified of Trevor as well as terrified of the consequences of her part in all this, whatever that part actually turned out to be. The only way they were going to get anything coherent out of the maid was if she managed to calm her down and did the questioning herself.

So she did.

"Slow down, Clara," she told her gently, then urged, "Take a breath." She waited until Clara complied. Aware that Trevor was all but chomping at the bit beside her, she still went slowly, her words emerging far more slowly than she would have wanted them to. But this was for the greater good. "Who are you talking about, Clara? Who's *him?*"

"Duke." Clara all but choked out the name in a whisper.

"Duke Johnson?" Trevor asked, stunned. Duke was one of the regulars who'd been on the ranch longer than he had. His suspicions had been focused on some of the newer hands, not Duke. He felt his temper mounting. If that cowboy had played him…

Clara avoided Trevor's eyes, staring down at her hands instead as she nodded.

It took her a moment but Gabby recalled what Clara had initially told them when they'd questioned her. She'd upheld Duke's alibi that he had spent that morning with her.

"So Duke really wasn't with you?" Gabby pressed, trying to get the story straight.

Clara was close to tears as she moved her head from side to side. "No, ma'am."

Trevor was through sitting on the sidelines, waiting for Gabby to work her way up to getting an answer out of a girl who looked as if she was afraid of her own shadow. "And where exactly *was* Duke, since he wasn't with you?" he asked gruffly.

Clara raised her head, her eyes all but pleading with him to understand why she'd done what she had. "I'm very, very sorry—" she began.

"Where was he?" Trevor asked again, enunciating each word carefully as his face all but turned a bright shade of red.

Incredibly nervous now, Clara hiccuped before answering. "He told me he was buying some drugs at the time—he's got this awful pain in his back, you see, and he can't get the doc to write him any more scripts for it, but he knows this man who knows this other man who can get them—"

She sounded as if she were winding up for an incredibly long explanation now that she'd finally got started. Trevor held his hand up to get the maid to stop before she went off on the completely wrong track. "And that's where he was during the time in question?" he demanded. "Buying drugs?"

"Yes, sir." Clara's head bobbed up and down several times like an over-energized bobblehead stuck on the dashboard. "He was afraid you'd fire him if you found out—or worse, that you'd think he was lying about where he was.

"But he swears he didn't have anything to do with your baby being kidnapped, Mr. Trevor. He just has all this pain sometimes, and—" Her voice cracked as she looked frantically from one to the other, apologies flowing from her lips like water through a crack in the dam. "I'm sorry, Mr. Trevor, Ms. Gabby, really sorry. I didn't want to lie to you. You've always been nothing but kind to me," she said, addressing the words to Gabby. "It's just that I didn't want Duke to be fired—or arrested," she added as the horrifying thought hit her. "Duke told me he was going to marry me just before this all happened. But he can't marry me if he's got no job."

Trevor was still chewing on the information he'd just learned, trying to come to grips with the idea that the kidnapper was someone he wouldn't have suspected.

Hell, he would have thought Mathilda Perkins capable of kidnapping his daughter before he would have laid the blame at Duke Johnson's doorstep. The wrangler had been a hand on the ranch for a lot of years.

A *hell* of a lot of years.

As for being a good worker, Duke was fair to middling, and he was far from conscientious, but as far as he knew, the wrangler was honest.

Duke *really* didn't seem to be the stealing type.

But almost anyone had his price. Apparently, the ransom he would have got had he taken the right child would have gone a long way to meeting Duke's price—whatever that was.

"Do you know where he is now?" Trevor demanded, his eyes all but trapping Clara.

She'd gone from being nervous and uncomfortable to being terrified. "He's supposed to be helping with the fences," she said, stuttering through some of the words. "He told me he might not be around for a while. Fixing fences is an all-day job. Sometimes two."

Trevor nodded. The foremen could give him a more accurate account of where the ranch hand was currently supposed to be.

If Duke believed himself to be safe, there was no reason to suppose he wasn't exactly where he was supposed to be. At least for the time being.

"Am I in trouble?" Clara asked, looking from him to Gabby and wringing her hands so hard it looked as though she were about to twist them off at the wrists. "I didn't want to lie, really I didn't, not to you. But I had no choice. I didn't want Duke to lose his job. He'd have to leave this area if he couldn't find work."

Or if he was arrested, Trevor couldn't help thinking. "I'm not in charge of hiring or firing anyone," he told her sternly. He felt sorry for her, but at the same time, he didn't like being lied to. The woman had cost them precious time. Time that could still mean the difference between life and death for his daughter. "That's not my department," he bit off, then nodded in Gabby's direction. "Ms. Colton's got more to say about that sort of thing than I do."

"Am I going to be fired?" Clara turned her terrified eyes toward Gabby.

"No, you're not fired," Gabby said. "But you should have told us the truth right away."

Clara gulped, relieved and yet still afraid. "I know, miss, and I'm sorry, really sorry. But—"

Gabby held her hand up, determined to stop the flow of words before she drowned in them.

"Yes, I know," she said. "Believe me, I know," she emphasized.

Anything not to be subjected to the torrent of words again.

Chapter 16

"Nope, haven't seen Duke. He's supposed to be here, but..." the foreman, Gray Stark, shrugged his shoulders in response to Trevor's question when the latter asked about Duke's whereabouts.

The foreman and Stewie Runyon, another wrangler, were both out on the range, working to mend a section of the fence that had sorely needed replacing since a particularly bad late-winter storm had hit it several months ago, chewing that length up rather badly.

"He didn't come out with us," Runyon said, adding his voice to Stark's. "This still about Faye's murder?" he asked, no doubt curious as to what would bring the head of security and Colton's youngest daughter out here just to talk to them.

"Either one of you know where he is or where he

could be?" Trevor asked, looking from Runyon back to Stark. He knew both men, liked both men as much as he was able to like anyone. He knew each to be a hard worker, though Runyon's background was still somewhat in doubt. He'd just showed up one day, looking for work, promising to work hard. So far, he hadn't broken his promise.

As to the foreman, Stark had grown up on the ranch and was the son of the last foreman, working his way up and taking over when his father passed away suddenly. Of the two, Stark was the one with a concrete alibi. He was performing as a bull rider at the rodeo and was in plain sight the entire time that the murder/kidnapping had taken place.

In response to his last question, both shook their heads. Gabby noticed that Runyon avoided making eye contact as he disavowed any knowledge of the missing hand's whereabouts.

"If you had to make a guess," Gabby said, speaking up and breaking her own promise to herself to let Trevor handle all the questioning, "where would you *guess* that he was?"

"I don't know, Ms. Colton," Runyon murmured to the tips of his boots.

"Just take a wild guess," Gabby coaxed, doing her best to encourage the wrangler. "No points taken off if you're wrong," she added with a warm smile.

The ranch hand scratched his dirty-blond hair. It was a toss-up whether he was thinking or just stalling for time before he came up with an answer.

"Johnson likes to hang around that maid, Clara something-or-other," he finally volunteered.

They already knew that, Gabby thought, feeling somewhat frustrated. "Her last name's Peterson," she told Runyon matter-of-factly.

"We've already talked to her," Trevor added. "She's the one who told us that he was supposed to be working out here."

"*Supposed* to be," Stark repeated, adding emphasis to the first word. "Doesn't mean that he would, though." Because the boss's daughter was there, the foreman appeared to bite back a few choice words of complaint. "He's been acting pretty strange these last few days," he told Trevor.

"Exactly how many days?" Trevor asked.

When Stark looked as if he was trying to understand exactly what Trevor was after, Gabby interrupted by saying, "Like, was it around the rodeo, before the rodeo, after the rodeo..."

She let her voice trail off, waiting for the foreman to jump in and clarify his statement for them.

"Before," Stark answered without any sort of hesitation. "Definitely before."

"Okay." Trevor nodded, accepting the foreman's reply. "How long 'before'?"

By now, both the foreman and Runyon had temporarily abandoned any pretense of working on the fence and instead focused on this far-more-interesting pursuit. The two men exchanged looks, as if silently trying to arrive at an agreement.

Runyon was the first to speak up. "I'd say maybe just before—say, a day."

But Stark shook his head. "It was more like two," he contradicted.

Runyon was silent for a moment, staring into the foreman's eyes, as if checking out the man's mindset. And then he relented.

"Yeah, I guess it was like that. Closer to two," the wrangler confirmed. He paused for a moment, as if debating.

"You think Johnson had something to do with taking your baby?" he finally asked.

"That's what we're trying to find out," Gabby replied, stepping in when Trevor appeared to be preoccupied with maintaining his silence, leaving the question unanswered.

"That means he would have had to have killed Ms. Faye," Runyon realized, startled by the connection he'd just made. "He wouldn't have done that," he declared with feeling. "Duke liked her," he stressed, then added, "We all did."

"Well, somebody sure didn't," Trevor reminded the two men grimly. He looked from one to the other and saw that both had told him all they knew—or at least all they *thought* they knew. "You boys think of anything else, you know how to reach me," he told them. Then, looking at Gabby, he said, "Let's go."

Gabby fell into step without a word. It was only once they had left the two wranglers to get back to their work did she ask, "Where are we going?" She lengthened her stride to keep up with Trevor as they returned to where he'd left his truck.

The way he saw it, since they were still trying to locate Johnson, there was only one logical answer to her question. "Back to the house to talk to that girlfriend of his again."

When they'd questioned Clara, she'd been fairly certain that the maid had told them all she knew. That didn't seem to be the case anymore. "You think she's holding something back?" Gabby asked him.

Trevor answered her honestly rather than just putting her off. "Dunno. But I intend to find out." And then he did something out of character. He shared something with Gabby rather than just keeping it to himself the way he usually did. "I've got a feeling about Duke," he told her just as they reached his truck.

"A bad feeling?" she asked, watching his expression as she got into the truck.

Trevor slid in behind the steering wheel before answering. "Let's just call it a gut feeling," he countered, recalling that she'd said she thought people in his line of work tended to have them.

Thinking back to when he'd initially questioned Johnson, he realized that the man's answers had been too pat, as though he'd practiced them first before he'd said them out loud.

At the time he hadn't paid much attention to that, since he'd known the man for more than five years. Now that he thought about it, he knew he should have gone along with the old cliché about trusting no one.

Especially since that was the usual way that he proceeded.

"You think Duke did it, don't you?" Gabby pressed, breaking the silence as Trevor pushed his truck, driving back to the house.

He never liked pinning himself down until he was absolutely sure about taking the course of action that he did. So he left his reply deliberately vague.

"I think that Johnson's involved somehow" was all he was willing to commit himself to.

Gabby sighed, reading between the lines. Why wouldn't Trevor just come out and *say* he suspected Johnson? It wasn't as if they were on opposite sides of a bet.

"You know," she pointed out, "there's no penalty payment if you're wrong."

"You're wrong there," he told her quietly, never taking his eyes off the road, despite the fact that the odds of seeing another vehicle were rather small.

She didn't quite understand what he was saying. "How do you figure that?"

He spelled it out for her. "If I'm wrong, if I wind up spinning my wheels by going in the wrong direction, I might wind up being too late. Avery might wind up paying the ultimate price," he added grimly.

For just a moment, Gabby could feel her heart constricting in her chest. But, battling that, once again she forced herself to think only positive thoughts. Negative ones sapped her strength and did nothing to help the situation a single bit. If anything, negative thoughts actually hindered it.

"We're going to find her," she told Trevor with a fierceness he would have found convincing if he weren't such a lifelong pessimist.

But rather than agree with her, he said the only thing he could have, given the situation. "I hope you're right, Gabriella."

"I am," she replied with a quiet conviction he found himself envying.

What made someone like Gabby the way she was? Granted, she was better off than most with no need to worry about mundane issues like paying off overdue bills, but she had an overbearing, womanizing father in the picture to balance everything out and to remind her that no matter who she was, there were dues to pay.

In an absolute sense, he supposed that, given everything, he was better off than she was.

Trevor parked his truck toward the rear of the house. It was closer to the wing that he and the other staff members who lived on the premises occupied.

As he got out, his attention was entirely focused on finding Clara and grilling the young woman. He hoped there was something she'd unintentionally omitted that just might help them find Johnson. He had a hunch that Johnson was the key to both the murder and his daughter's kidnapping.

The thought that the wrangler had panicked and taken off was something he didn't want to contemplate just yet, since if he had, finding Avery was going to become more difficult by at least a hundredfold.

One step at a time, he reminded himself. *A man can take only one step at a time.*

"Soon as I talk to that girl, I've got a feeling we'll be taking off again," he said to Gabby, "so you can stay in the truck if you want."

But she had already got out of the truck. "The hell I will," she informed him defiantly. She was not about to just sit around, twiddling her thumbs, waiting for him to find the next clue. "Besides, you need me with you when you talk to Clara," she pointed out, adding, "You scare her."

The barest hint of a smile creased his lips. "I don't scare you," he noted.

He had, in the beginning, but she'd got past that, and besides, there was no way she was going to admit that to him, at least, not for a long time.

"We Colton women are a heartier bree—"

Gabby didn't get a chance to finish her sentence as a sound that resembled a car backfiring pierced the air. The next second, it became clear that what she'd heard was actually a gun being fired. The realization occurred at the same time that she'd felt something close to her cheek. A fly? God forbid it was a moth.

She automatically touched her face just as Trevor came flying across the front hood of the truck and literally tackled her. Her head would have hit the ground if he hadn't been as fast as he was, cradling the back of her head as she went down under him.

The air was knocked out of her lungs, and it took her more than a minute to finally be able to speak. "What are yo—?"

"Quiet!" Trevor ordered, straining to hear any tell-tale noises coming from the surrounding area. His body might have been on top of hers, but his attention was completely focused on locating the source of the gun-fire. He concluded in a matter of seconds that the shot had come from somewhere in the house.

That left him a hell of a lot of territory to cover and a wealth of people to hold suspect.

His service revolver drawn, Trevor was ready to re-turn fire if it came to that. But beyond the single shot, no more bullets were fired.

"You all right?" he finally asked, sparing her a quick glance before scanning the immediate area again.

"Having a little trouble breathing right now," she told him. And she was. It was hard drawing air in with what amounted to having a lead weight on her body.

Concern instantly creased his features. "Where are you hit?" Trevor asked.

"I'm not hit," she informed him. Didn't the man see why she was having so much trouble breathing? Was he completely oblivious to her problem? "You're on top of me, and it might be all pure muscle, but it's also very *heavy* muscle," she said, trying vainly to catch her breath.

He felt almost like someone waking up out of a night-mare. Trevor rolled off Gabby quickly, then offered her his hand to help her up.

Gabby had no issues with accepting his hand or his help. That sort of pride was merely empty pride. Taking his hand, she gained her feet. That was when she saw the look of concern on his face intensify.

"What?" she asked.

"You're hit," he cried, stunned and deeply worried at the same time. He tilted up her head toward the sun for a better view. And then she saw his features relax just a shade. Which meant that it couldn't have been as bad as they'd thought. "The bullet just grazed you," he confirmed.

"Grazed is good, right?" she asked him, to confirm her innocent belief.

"Yeah, grazed is good—especially when you consider the alternative," Trevor allowed. Right now, he was fighting an overwhelming desire just to take her into his arms and hold her to assure himself that she was really all right.

By now, the main nanny, Mathilda Perkins, as well as several of the maids—including Clara—had come running out of the house once they saw what was happening, and now they surrounded both of them, as if they intended on acting like human shields.

"My God, Ms. Colton, you're hurt," Mathilda cried, staring at the bloodied area along her cheek. The older woman's chest was heaving and her hand was splayed across it, like someone who was trying to keep their heart from leaping out of their chest.

"It's just a flesh wound," Gabby told the woman, brushing off the very visible problem. She grinned at

Trevor. "When I was a little girl, I always wanted to say that."

"You were a very strange little girl," he pronounced, doing his best to mask the surge of both fear and affection he was presently experiencing. Fear because the gunshot could have been a great deal more serious if it had been fired just eighteen inches lower.

Trevor thought of going into the house and searching for the shooter, but it was obvious, since the gunfire had ceased after the first round had gone off, that whoever had fired at Gabby—if she *had* been the actual target—was gone. Otherwise, there would have been more bullets flying about.

Someone was trying to make a point, send a message. But what, and who? He didn't feel any closer to finding the answers than he had earlier.

If the shooter had been Duke, then the wrangler was taking one hell of a chance. While the barely-out-of-adolescence womanizer seemed to be the prime candidate in the abduction, he was really not the sharpest knife in the drawer. And he didn't really see the wrangler as being capable of murder—and that included shooting at Gabby.

Someone else besides Duke had to be involved, Trevor thought.

"When I heard that gunshot, I was afraid that someone else had been killed," Mathilda was saying. "Come, let me take you inside and take care of that," the nanny urged Gabby.

But the latter glanced in Trevor's direction and shook

her head. She had a feeling that Trevor was going to take off the minute he finished talking to Clara. She had no intentions of remaining behind.

"There's no time for that now," she said. Pulling a handkerchief out of her back pocket, she quickly dabbed at her cheek. "There, all done," she declared.

"It's a far cry from being taken care of," the older woman replied reprovingly. But Gabby chose to ignore Mathilda for the time being.

Trevor had cornered Clara and was taking her aside to question. She needed to get in on this, Gabby thought. What she'd said earlier to Trevor wasn't something she was attempting to brag about. She was serious. She had a feeling that Clara would be far less frightened and more forthcoming with her around.

"Does he have any special place he likes to go?" she heard Trevor asking the maid as she crossed to the duo. "Somewhere the two of you can be alone?" he pressed. Both she and Duke had quarters within the appropriate wings that they shared. That made achieving any sort of intimacy difficult.

"Well, he does have this little place," Clara admitted with a dismissive shrug. "It's not much and it's kind of run-down."

Right now, he didn't need a description; he needed an address.

"Where?" Trevor implored, doing his best to keep from shouting the word at the maid. She seemed exceedingly flustered, yet eager to please at the same time.

Clara continued to make excuses, as if the apartment

and its locale somehow reflected on her. "It's not really in the best part of town—"

His temper was all but frayed, and she was sorely trying what was left. *"Where is it?"*

The moment Clara rattled off the address, he was off and running again.

When he realized that Gabby was hurrying to keep up with him, he didn't slow down. Instead, he shouted an order at her. "Stay here, damn it. Have that cheek taken care of."

That was *not* about to stop her. "My cheek is fine. You need someone to watch your back," she countered, raising her voice so he could hear her as he hurried.

There was no way she could hope to live up to that. Trevor pointed out the obvious. "You can't 'watch my back.' You don't have a gun."

That didn't worry her. There were lots of guns to be had where they were going. *If* they had to go that far to get one—which she doubted.

"You probably have an extra one either strapped on you somewhere or in the truck. I do know how to shoot a gun," she informed him. "You can't grow up around these parts and not know your way around a gun."

He couldn't picture her firing a weapon. "If I find out that you're lying—"

"You won't," she told him confidently as she quickly got into the truck and buckled up.

She said that with confidence, but he didn't know if she meant that she *could* shoot a gun or that she didn't intend for him to find out that she couldn't.

In either case, the woman was incredibly feisty, and even when she infuriated him, he couldn't help but admire her at the same time.

Gabriella Colton, he caught himself thinking as he pressed down harder on the accelerator, was really one hell of a woman and so much more than he'd initially thought.

He found the realization comforting beyond words. Not to mention oddly arousing.

For the time being, he tucked the second feeling away.

Chapter 17

Rising anticipation mixed with adrenaline had Gabby holding her breath as she and Trevor drew closer to the building where Duke Johnson was said to maintain his other living quarters.

Just as Clara had told them, the neighborhood appeared to be less than thriving and was definitely run-down-looking.

Trevor slanted a glance in Gabby's direction just as they turned a corner and arrived at their destination. He could see by her expression that she was surprised the wrangler would have chosen a place like this to serve as his hideaway or, since bedding women apparently was his hobby of choice, as a so-called love nest.

He judged that a woman of Gabby's background and breeding wasn't even aware that run-down, most likely vermin-infested places like this actually existed outside of a movie set.

"Not what you expected, eh?" he speculated.

A long moment stretched out between them and then she merely shrugged. When she spoke, he had to strain to hear her. Her voice had dropped by several octaves.

"I'm not really sure exactly what I expected. Right now, all I'm hoping for is that we find Duke, and that he can tell us where we can find Avery."

"You don't have to whisper," Trevor said, trying to figure out why she'd lowered her voice to such a degree when she answered him. "Johnson's a ranch hand, not some superhero with super hearing."

"I know that," she muttered, feeling as if the rest of her nerves were eroding. What she didn't know was whether or not the wrangler they were looking for was still here, in his poor excuse of an apartment, or if he'd already packed up his few possessions and vanished, taking Avery with him if indeed he'd stolen the infant in the first place.

Trevor opened the vehicle door on his side, then paused to look at her over his shoulder. "If I tell you to stay in the truck, would you listen?"

Despite her accommodating nature, she had never taken orders well. Now was no exception. As far as she was concerned, she had a vested interest in finding Avery. Aside from everything else, she was falling in love with Avery's father.

"No."

Trevor sighed, shaking his head. "I didn't think

so." He closed his door. "Guess I should just save my breath."

She got out on the passenger side. "Guess so," she agreed.

Being torn between wanting to strangle Gabby and wanting to hug her was becoming almost commonplace for him.

They made their way quickly and soundlessly into the run-down apartment building.

Johnson's so-called alternate quarters were located on the fourth floor. There was no elevator. The stairs between the floors were badly in need of washing.

"Still with me?" Trevor asked as they came to the third-floor landing.

"Haven't lost me yet," she answered, although— maybe because of the graze she'd received earlier— her legs felt somewhat rubbery. But by the time they came to the fourth floor, she was experiencing a sudden surge of energy coursing through her veins. She chalked it up to more adrenaline.

Trevor waved her behind him as he approached the missing ranch hand's apartment door.

Rather than argue the point or ignore the silent instruction, Gabby did as he indicated. Her entire focus was on getting this over with and, hopefully, finding Avery. Arguing would only slow them down.

Instead of knocking, Trevor took out what appeared to be a skeleton key and jimmied the lock open. Done, he pocketed the key and took out his gun. Realistically, he had very little hope of finding Johnson on the premises, but there was always a chance that, for once, things were going his way.

Apparently things *were* going his way.

When he eased the door open as soundlessly as possible, Trevor found himself looking at Johnson's back. The wrangler was bending over, occupied with whatever was on the sofa. He also appeared to be saying something, but his voice wasn't nearly loud enough, and his words, for the most part, went unheard.

Gabby thought she made out the phrase "Gotta go now," but she wasn't sure.

When Duke turned around, he was holding a bundle in his arms.

Avery.

"One more trip, then it's the end of the line for you," the wrangler was saying to the infant he was holding.

Gabby thought her heart would burst right then and there. They'd found not only the missing wrangler, but, far more important, they'd found Avery. Even at this distance, she could recognize the sleeper the infant was wearing. It was the same one Avery had had on when she'd put the little girl down in Cheyenne's crib a week ago.

"Hold it right there, Johnson," Trevor ordered. The gun in his hand was aimed at the other man and it underscored his command.

Johnson instantly tightened his arms around the baby to such a degree that the infant began to cry. Panic was written all over the twenty-two-year-old blond wrangler's face.

"You wouldn't risk killing your own kid, would you, Mr. Garth?" Duke asked nervously, shifting the baby so that she was in front of him, her body shielding some of his more vital organs.

"Nope, I sure wouldn't," Trevor replied calmly. "I'm a hell of a lot better shot than that." There was no bravado in his words. He had just simply stated a fact. It was no secret around Dead River that the head of security was a crack marksman.

There was less than a minute's debate before Johnson lowered the child and surrendered. The moment he did, Gabby swooped in, taking the baby from him and cradling the infant against her.

"It's over, sweetheart," she cooed to the baby. "You're going home."

Trevor was instantly on the wrangler's other side, pulling Johnson's arms behind his back and handcuffing him.

"I'm sorry, Mr. Garth—I really, truly am," Johnson cried. "I didn't know it was your baby until it was too late. You've always been good to me, and if I'd known it was her lying there, I wouldn't have taken her. I swear I wouldn't have."

Trevor yanked Johnson's hands together harder as he cuffed him, struggling to hold on to his temper. "Tell that to Faye."

"I'm sorry about her, too." Johnson was nearly crying now. "I didn't want to hurt her."

"You did a damn sight more than that to her," Trevor bit off. "You killed her."

Johnson tried to make Trevor understand how things had got completely out of hand. "She didn't give me no choice. She was gonna call the chief, turn me in."

"You were kidnapping someone's baby—that's the kind of thing you've got to expect." Trevor's voice was emotionless as he said the words.

Duke Johnson had had a run-in with the law once or twice as a kid, but after that, his record had been completely clean. This complete about-face of his didn't make any sense. "Why you do it?" Trevor wanted to know.

"Money," Duke answered simply with a vague shrug. Then he specified the amount, as if that explained it all. "I was promised ten thousand dollars." That was a lot of money to someone who didn't have any. "All I had to do was kidnap your niece, hold her for ransom, then leave the money in an envelope right here on the table. Easy." He laughed shortly. "How was I to know that you'd switched babies on me?" he complained. "They all look alike."

Trevor looked around the apartment. A man with money didn't stay in a place like this. "Where's the money?" he asked.

"Wasn't any," Johnson lamented. "I took the wrong kid, remember?"

Trevor's eyes narrowed. "Who ordered the kidnapping?"

Johnson's wide shoulders rose and fell in another hapless shrug. "I dunno."

Trevor's temper flared. What was the wrangler trying

to pull? "What do you mean you don't know? Someone had to tell you to kidnap Jethro Colton's granddaughter. Who was it?" Trevor growled. He was swiftly reaching the end of his patience, and with everything he'd been put through this past week, he hadn't had much to start with.

Afraid, Johnson's voice rose an octave as he repeated, "I don't know. Someone slipped a note under my door at Dead River, telling me what they wanted me to do and what they'd pay me to do it." He pressed his lips together nervously, his eyes shifting to Gabby, silently begging her to intercede on his behalf. "When I took the wrong baby, I found another note saying I wasn't going to get a dime and to get rid of the kid as soon as possible."

"Why didn't you just return her?" Gabby wanted to know.

But Johnson was shaking his head. "I was afraid someone would see me."

"So you were going to keep her?" she asked, trying to understand what the ranch hand had been thinking.

"Well, I thought about it," Johnson admitted, but then said, "but what's a ranch hand supposed to do with a kid?"

Hearing his former sentiments repeated like this made Trevor angry with both himself as well as with Duke. "So what were your plans?" Trevor demanded, his tone dark and foreboding.

"Well, there're all these people out there, looking to adopt a little baby, so I thought I'd just sell her to the highest bidder." Suddenly Johnson found himself being lifted up by his throat, his feet doing a frantic dance as he vainly searched for solid ground. "Or maybe not," he croaked out hoarsely, desperate to get Trevor to put him down again.

"Trevor, please, put him down," Gabby pleaded. "He's not worth it."

Trevor debated his course of action a moment longer, then reluctantly released the wrangler.

When he did, Johnson began to cough fitfully, trying to catch his breath again. When he did, he apologized profusely again.

"Look, I'm sorry, but you never wanted her anyway, so I thought maybe if I found some family that did, she'd be okay. It just made sense, right?"

Guilt skewered him. He struggled to bank it down.

He'd made serious mistakes, Trevor silently admitted, but he was getting another chance to make things right. He fully intended to do just that.

"Don't go giving yourself a halo just yet," Trevor growled at the handcuffed wrangler. "I want her, and you almost cost me my daughter."

With Johnson securely handcuffed and too afraid to move, Trevor turned his attention to his rescued infant daughter.

Gabby was still holding her, but the moment she saw the look in his eyes, she handed the baby over to Trevor without a word.

"Hi," Trevor whispered to the infant. He didn't trust his voice not to break if he spoke any louder. Avery stopped fussing for a moment and stared at him as if he was the most fascinating creature in her world. Even so, she was still trying to fit her fist into her mouth. "Remember me? I'm your daddy. Haven't been much of one up to now," he admitted. "But all that's going to change, as of right now," he promised earnestly.

Gabby thought her heart was going to burst right then and there. She felt tears stinging her eyes and blinked hard to keep them from falling. She had a feeling that happy tears were beyond Trevor's realm of comprehension.

"I'll call the chief," she volunteered, her throat thick with emotion. "You just get reacquainted with your daughter."

"Why is she shoving her fist into her mouth?" Trevor asked just as she opened her phone.

"That means she's hungry. Check the refrigerator, see if there's any formula in there," she told him, then raised her voice as he left the room with his daughter so she could add, "and don't forget to warm it up!"

"I'm not an idiot," Trevor responded.

"No," she murmured under her breath. "Just a newbie father."

But from the looks of it, he'd be a doting one, Gabby thought fondly as she continued looking in his direction even though Trevor was in the kitchen now.

"Looks like you did my work for me," the chief said less than twenty minutes later after he had been filled in on what had happened.

His gaze took in Johnson and it was obvious that the older man was sorely disappointed. He had been the one to vouch for Duke, acting as a reference when Duke was looking to be hired at Dead River. For the most part, Johnson had been a hard worker. But the homicide—accidental or not—and kidnapping changed everything.

"Not quite," Trevor replied grimly to the chief's comment. "We still don't know who put the word out to have Cheyenne Colton kidnapped." He glanced in Gabby's direction. She'd taken the baby from him again, freeing him up to talk to the chief unencumbered. "Which means that your niece's life still might be in danger," he told her.

"Whoever's behind the first kidnapping could have just cut his losses and taken off," the chief pointed out.

That seemed way too optimistic to him, Trevor thought. Revenge or money—either way the kidnapper hadn't got what he was after.

"Better safe than sorry," he told the police chief, then turned back to Gabby. "I'm hiring a bodyguard for your niece."

His words were met with a smile. They were of like mind: better safe than sorry. "Sounds good to me," Gabby told him. "I'm sure Amanda will say the same thing," she added.

"I'll come on out to the ranch to do some more nosing around," the chief told Trevor. "Just as soon as I get this one behind bars," he added, indicating the handcuffed wrangler.

Johnson had the look of a desperate man as the reality of the situation—and its consequences—were beginning to sink in. "I didn't mean to kill Ms. Faye. She just kept coming at me," Johnson cried. "It was an accident."

The chief paused to look disdainfully now at the young man he'd once trusted. "Whether you meant it or not, Faye's still dead," he pointed out.

Johnson made a desperate, unintelligible noise.

"One question," Trevor said, holding a hand up and getting in Johnson's way as the chief began to lead him out of the room.

Johnson looked at him warily, as if he was expecting some sort of trap. "Yeah?"

"How did you get back to your apartment so fast?" he asked.

Johnson stared at him, not comprehending the question. "What do you mean?"

Trevor knew the difference when someone was playing dumb. Johnson appeared genuinely confused. "Back at the ranch, when we went to talk to Clara again, you took a shot at Ms. Colton—"

The wrangler looked horrified. To kill a staff member was one thing. To kill one of the Coltons carried with it far darker penalties.

"No, I didn't," Johnson protested. "I've been here since last night, trying to figure out what to do with the kid. Someone shot at you?" Johnson asked, looking uncertainly at Gabby.

In response, Trevor gently turned her cheek toward the handcuffed wrangler, letting him see the grazed mark. "Sure looks like it, doesn't it?"

The news was a revelation to the chief as well. He seemed rather upset by this newest twist. "You want to come down and make a statement, Ms. Colton?" he asked Gabby.

But Gabby shook her head. "Later," she answered. "Right now, all I'd like to do is get this little one back home and change her." She lightly patted the baby's rather soggy bottom. Avery was in desperate need of a fresh diaper, not to mention a clean outfit. "My guess is that, right now, she's about twice her normal weight."

"At your convenience, then," the chief said politely, tipping his hat to her. His face clouded over as he turned his attention back to his prisoner. "Move, boy," he ordered gruffly.

"Okay," Trevor said once the other two had departed from the old apartment, "it's time to get my girls home."

Startled, Gabby's head jerked up, and she looked at him closely, as if to scrutinize him. "You must really be tired," she concluded.

He felt far too wired at the moment to be even remotely tired. "What makes you say that?"

Wasn't it obvious to him? Or hadn't he heard himself just now? "Because you just referred to both of us as 'your girls.'"

Trevor looked at her, waiting. He still didn't see what the problem was. "So?"

"Well," she explained slowly, "Avery's your girl because she's your daughter...." Her voice trailed off after that, giving him space to draw his conclusion from what she'd just eluded to.

The light dawned. "And you don't want to be."

That wasn't what she was saying. "No. Yes." And then she came to a skidding halt. "Wait a minute—are you actually calling me that on purpose?"

"You don't like it," he guessed. Was she one of those women who took a term of endearment and only saw it as an insult?

"I didn't say that," she told him, trying to pin him down.

Okay, she'd just lost him, he thought. "Then what did you say?"

Gabby countered his question with one of her own. "What are *you* saying?"

Taking a deep breath, he backtracked. "You're asking me to spell it out?"

She felt her pulse accelerating again, except that this time, there were no guns involved, no kidnappers around. This was just two people, dancing around the right words and a time-old tradition that had yet to be set in motion.

"I think you're going to have to, otherwise, I'm just going to think one of us is hallucinating," she answered.

He supposed, after everything she'd gone through for him, she had this coming. He took a second to pull himself together and get his thoughts right.

"I didn't think it was possible at my age," Trevor began, "but you've managed to make me see things differently, to see things in a better light than I ever have before...."

She did her best not to look amused. "So far, you're

making me sound like I was some kind of a fledgling saint."

That was *not* his intent. "Not really. I don't think a saint, fledgling or not, would have done the kind of things you did the other night." This time, there was no muting his smile. It spread out all over his face.

"Now you're making me sound like some kind of a sinner," she pointed out.

He shook his head, vetoing the second image. "What you are, Gabby, is the total package. A saint and a sinner, all rolled up into one. What I'd like to know..."

For a moment, the sentence just hung there, unfinished, so she prodded. "Yes?"

He began again, his mouth so dry he was afraid his tongue was going to stick to the roof of his mouth if he didn't get all this out soon. "What I'd like to know is if you'd like to be my personal saint/sinner."

That sounded like a requisition for a job. "What's that supposed to mean?"

He blew out an impatient breath. Why was this so hard? "I'm trying to ask you to marry me."

"Then ask me to marry you," she suggested. "Don't talk in riddles."

Trevor tried again, hoping this time it would come out right. "Gabriella Colton—"

"You usually call me Gabby," she reminded him. Things were comfortably informal between them now. She didn't want to lose that.

Nervous, Trevor was swiftly becoming exasperated. "Will you stop interrupting?"

"Okay." But then she began to say something more.

Trevor put his finger to her lips to keep her from saying anything further before he got this out. "Gabby Colton, will you do me the supreme honor of becoming my wife?"

As far as proposals went, this one certainly lacked feeling, never mind passion. So she asked, "Why?"

He could only stare at her, dumbfounded. "What do you mean 'why?'"

"Well, if you want me to marry you, there has to be a reason. Are you asking me to marry you because you like the way I cook—? Wait, you've never eaten anything I've cooked, so it's not that. Is it the way I diaper a baby? Because you've seen me do that. Or is it—?"

Not knowing how else to make her stop talking, he shouted over her. "I'm asking you to marry me because I love you!"

She smiled contentedly then, like a cat that had got into a case full of cream. "There, now was that really so hard?" she asked him sweetly.

They weren't officially engaged yet and already she had him jumping through hoops, he thought. "Damn it, woman, you're going to make me crazy."

She grinned up at him. "You ain't seen nothin' yet, Trevor Garth."

He caught hold of her arms and pulled her closer, despite the fact that she was still holding his daughter, who was now fast asleep. "But I've got a feeling I'm going to," he replied. Then, before she could say another word, he leaned into her and kissed her.

Even with the baby between them, his kiss still rocked her world. And she had the feeling that it would continue to do so for a very long time.

Gabby couldn't wait to be proven right.

Epilogue

Gabby's bedroom—it was more like a suite, in his opinion—complete with a sitting room, was more than twice the size of his old quarters located in the staff's wing. Even with the crib she'd kept there initially for her niece, the crib that was now to accommodate Avery, the room was still huge. When the crib had been put in his room, there had barely been enough space to move around in.

From what he could see, Gabby could have had a small circus performing here—complete with baby elephants—and there still would have been room left over.

It had taken him a little more than two hours to gather together all of his things, as well as Avery's belongings, and bring them over to Gabby's room. She'd suggested, in light of recent events, that he move in with her. There was more than enough room in her walk-in closet for his clothes, the baby's few clothes and, most likely, the clothes of some small, fashion-minded Western European country.

Ordinarily utterly secure in his identity and in his abilities to handle any situation, Trevor was aware of battling feelings of inadequacy. He'd always been his own man—even before he'd actually *been* a man.

But even so, he looked around Gabby's room uncertainly.

"You're sure about this?" he asked. Gabby gazed at him questioningly, obviously waiting for him to elaborate, and he obliged. "About my moving in with you? Your father—"

Gabby saw where this was going and cut Trevor off before things could escalate and veer off in unstable directions.

"—has bigger things on his mind right now than you moving into my rooms," she assured him firmly. "Besides, you're not exactly some random lover I happened to stumble across at a saloon one night and decided to take to my bed. You're a brave, well-respected former police officer he handpicked to be head of his ranch's security. Plus you're my fiancé and you've vowed to make an honest woman out of me, remember?" she reminded him.

Moving closer, Gabby placed her hand on his chest,

her fingers splaying out playfully along the ridges and muscles she felt beneath her palm.

"It's okay," she told him with feeling as well as a sexy smile on her lips.

He laughed and closed his arms around Gabby, drawing her closer to him. Close enough to feel her heart beating in rhythm with his.

Such a small sound, generating such a comforting feeling, he couldn't help thinking.

"Honest woman," he echoed with a small laugh. "It's you who's making an honest man out of me." He saw her brow furrow slightly in confusion, so he explained. "Before you came into my life, I figured I was just meant to drift through life, standing on the outside, looking in, seeing other people enjoying themselves, having all the normal things everyone wants—a home, a family. Love. Things I never had, thought I was never *going* to have. But you changed all that. You made all that happen," he told her.

He could feel his heart swelling with love as well as gratitude—gratitude for so many things.

"And maybe I don't show it, and maybe there'll be times when I won't act it, but I'm going on the record here and now, Gabby, to say that I know how very lucky I am and how much I appreciate you loving me."

A teasing smile played along her lips. "Oh, you do, now, do you?"

But he didn't take the easy way out, didn't resort to teasing, abandoning the serious note the first moment he could because it embarrassed him. This had to be said—if only once—and he wanted her to know exactly what she meant to him.

"Yes, I do," he told her. "You saved me, Gabby. You saved me from becoming an unhappy, bitter man way before my time."

"So there's a time for you to become unhappy and bitter?" she pretended to ask innocently.

He laughed, capturing her lips for a fleeting moment and savoring the taste of her.

But he couldn't allow himself to get carried away. His daughter was in her crib, which was in the adjoining sitting room and out of sight, but he was still aware of her being there and possibly awake.

"You know what I mean," he said to Gabby. "I'm not very good at words."

"Oh, on the contrary," she said with conviction. "You're very good with words, Trevor." A wicked smile moved across her mouth as she went on to tell him, "But you're even better at something else."

"Oh?" He raised an eyebrow, as if to question her words. "And what would that be?"

Raising her head, she ever-so-faintly brushed her lips against his in what felt like almost a phantom kiss. And then she drew back, her eyes dancing.

"Guess."

"Okay," he answered gamely.

Pulling her in even closer, Trevor sealed his lips to hers. Just as he began to do so, he heard her sigh with anticipated contentment. "Right as usual."

He could feel her smile beneath his lips as they found hers. He didn't know about "usual," but he was damn glad he was right.

* * * * *

Don't miss the next story in
THE COLTONS OF WYOMING *miniseries:*
COLTON BY BLOOD
by Melissa Cutler,
available August 2013 from
Harlequin Romantic Suspense.
For a sneak peek, turn the page....

Chapter 1

You can't make peace with a ghost. Kate McCord knew this as fact.

It was one of those secrets of life that no one would tell you and you had to uncover for yourself, like discovering Santa Claus wasn't real. It stuck in Kate's craw, all the truths that nobody saw fit to share. She'd found out the hard way, and not until it was too late, that bankruptcy would not solve your problems, no matter how enthusiastically a lawyer told you it would, not all men cared if a woman orgasmed and croissants—the real kind, not the ones sold in supermarkets—were nearly a third butter.

And the memories of the people you loved and lost? Well, all they did was haunt.

It was dark in the servant stairwell. A sprawling,

fluid darkness that seeped into cracks and corners and right into Kate's skin. A dessert tray balanced on her right hand, heavy and ungainly. Her left hand pressed to the wall, holding her steady as she stood rooted on a stair somewhere between the first and second floors, at least ten steps in either direction to the nearest door. Too great a distance for a woman who was afraid of the dark.

She had no idea how long she'd been waiting for the power to be restored, but it had to have been well over five minutes, perhaps ten if the rising heat and stuffiness were any indication. The watch she wore had a light, but activating it would require her to set the tray down. Not only was the tray too large to balance on a step, but she wasn't sure she could convince her body to move.

Her pulse pounded all the way to the tips of her fingers and toes. Any second now, Horace or Jared or one of the other ranch hands would get the generator fired up and she'd be safe.

Any second now.

Every so often, distant voices cut through the unbearable silence that had replaced the hum of the air-conditioning system. Footsteps clomped away, fading off. Nobody ventured onto the stairs. All that mattered to the waitstaff was restoring the Colton family to the level of comfort to which they were accustomed. Locating a stranded cook's assistant probably didn't cross anyone's mind.

It would've crossed Faye's mind. She'd been Kate's closest friend at Dead River Ranch. In all of Wyoming, really. But Faye was gone, and now the kind old woman was yet another person Kate loved who'd died before their time only to haunt the shadows of her mind. Another ethereal face in the darkness.

She shivered.

The note she'd stuffed in her pocket in haste crackled. On the tray, the glass dish of bread pudding quivered.

Steady, Kate. It's only a power outage.

Maybe if she kept her focus on the pudding, she would survive this ordeal with her sanity intact. She'd spent hours on that dessert, baking the challah loaves, preparing the custard and whiskey sauce. It was a sumptuous creation topped by a pillow of fresh whipped cream. Mr. Colton's favorite sweet, if his frequent requests were any indication.

A boom of great force sounded from nearby. A door slamming or something hitting a wall. A tree falling, perhaps. Fierce wind storms were most likely to blame for the power outage. They'd plagued Western Wyoming for more than a week, beating on the ranch house and surrounding wilderness, unrelenting. Sinister.

Another hard truth Kate had discovered for herself was that Mother Nature was the greatest devil of all, an unremorseful murderer. Every time the weather turned nasty, the faces of William and baby Olive—and now Faye—hovered in the front of her mind.

She'd felt so safe at Dead River Ranch, where busy servants and the lazy, entitled family left the lights burning all day and night. The kitchen was her co-

coon. A warm, bright, safe place to call home. Until last month.

Poor Faye.

Murdered by the devil's lackey, a hired gun who'd been caught and locked away, though the mastermind behind the murder was still at large. The writer of the note in Kate's pocket. Someone who, she dreaded, remained on the ranch. Maybe someone she spoke to every day or whom she'd helped prepare meals for. Without money or anywhere else to go, her only two choices were to carry on with her job, hoping that law enforcement levied justice onto the devil behind Faye's death before more harm was done, or take matters into her own hands and do what she could to help the investigation.

The note was a testament to her efforts, not that anything had come of the stolen evidence. She'd nearly been caught red-handed tonight in the pantry by Fiona, and she could well imagine the repercussions of being caught with evidence she had no business possessing.

On one of the two floors above her, the stairwell door opened with a bang that made Kate gasp. The tray tilted perilously. She felt the shift of weight as the dish of pudding slid, the teacup, too.

Her gasp turned into a cry of panic as she bent her knees and crooked her elbows, willing the tray to level. No, no, no. Not the pudding.

But her correction was too severe, overcompensating for her first error. The tray lightened as the entirety of the contents crashed to the stairs in an explosion of shattering glass and clanging silver.

She squeezed her eyes closed and hugged the tray flat against her chest.

Agnes was going to be furious. Delivering dessert to Mr. Colton's sickbed was supposed to be the final task of her sixteen-hour workday. Fiona had asked the favor of her on the sly since they hadn't secured Agnes's permission. Kate wouldn't put it past the bitter-tempered head chef to demand Kate's dismissal, as she'd threatened to do almost daily since Kate took the assistant-cook job four years earlier.

The flicker of a moving flashlight accompanied hushed footsteps on the stairs above. Someone was moving through the dark in her direction. Wordlessly.

A savior or the devil?

Surrounded as she was by broken glass, she wouldn't have been able to move even if she could've convinced her feet to unstick from the ground. Even if she was able to decide if she should climb toward the person whose footsteps were getting louder and closer or if she should run away.

"Hello?" she whispered.

No answer.

She shuffled her feet backward, unintentionally kicking glass shards with her heels. With a tinkling sound, they tumbled down a step.

Light, either from a candle or flashlight, came into view on the stairs above her. Another door opened, this time from the ground floor, and with the new arrival, more glowing light. The descending footsteps grew louder, the wobbling light brighter.

Kate held her breath, too terrified to move. Damn the darkness and damn her crippling fear.

With a crack of surging electricity, the lights came on. Kate's relief was tempered by the sight on the landing above her of Mathilda holding a flashlight, her expression as severe as her black, high-collared dress. She held her lips in a pucker that drew attention to the numerous little wrinkles on her upper lip. "What on earth," she said with slow precision.

Strict but fair on the staff under her command, Mathilda had earned her position in the household through decades of devoted service. She ranked above every other member of the staff, yet the glass ceiling between her and the family was ever-present. Kate didn't envy her the loneliness of the position.

A rattle of dishes behind Kate preceded Agnes's grating voice. "Oh, Kate. What in the name of all things holy did you do, child?"

Kate bit her tongue against a retort. A child, she was not. A penniless widow, grieving mother and pastry chef, yes, but not a child. Not for a long time.

Twisting on the spot, she glanced at the dessert tray in Agnes's hands before fixing her gaze on the round woman's spiky, persimmon-red hair. "When the power went out, I slipped and the tray fell. There was nothing I could do."

A lie, but a necessary one. She had never dared confess her fear of the dark to anyone but dear, sweet Faye, and she certainly wasn't going to spill her soul for the Dragon Lady—the whispered nickname some of the staff used for Agnes. Kate didn't have much to call her own anymore but she still had her pride.

Without a word, Kate knelt and loaded the wreckage onto her tray.

"Look what you've done," Agnes clucked. "What a disaster." With every word, Agnes's voice climbed in both decibel and register. "Careless, is what you are. And where is Fiona?"

Kate opened her mouth, but spotted the note near Mathilda's shoe. It must have fallen out of her pocket when the tray tipped. She reached for it but Mathilda was quicker.

Her heart dropped to her stomach at the sight of Mathilda unfolding the paper.

"Is this what I think it is?" Mathilda asked. Her eyes darted as she read. "How did you…?"

On pure instinct, Kate reached for the paper, but Mathilda lifted it out of arm's reach.

"She looks guilty. What is it?" Agnes asked.

Mathilda looked over Kate's head at Agnes. "It appears to be a copy of the kidnapping-for-hire note." Returning her focus to Kate, she added, "Where did you get this?"

There was no good answer that excused her misconduct, or at least Kate wasn't clever enough to come up with one on the spot.

The real answer was that she'd brought a tray of sticky buns to the Dead Police Department under the ruse that it was a thank-you from the Colton family. While the officers indulged, Kate pilfered through the police file. Then while they washed the sticky syrup from their hands, she'd made a copy. She had no intention of revealing the truth, however. "I can't tell you that, but I swear I didn't mean any harm with it. I thought maybe I'd see something in the note to help the police. Faye deserves justice for what happened to her."

"Of course she does, dear. She was a darling woman and we all miss her terribly. I'm sure the police are doing all they can. The Coltons are working closely with them, as am I. There is no need to put yourself at risk unnecessarily." She returned the letter to Kate. "My advice—destroy this before it gets you into trouble."

"Yes, ma'am." She folded the paper and returned it to her pocket.

"Why do you also have a tray, Agnes?" Mathilda's tone was placating.

"Mr. Colton buzzed. He hadn't received his dessert yet and was in quite a state. That Fiona is a lazy one. Makes us all look bad. She probably would've stolen away to eat the sweets herself. Takes advantage, that girl. And you—" She leveled a sneer at Kate. "I have half a mind to fire you both."

Kate set the last manageable shard on the tray and straightened. The remaining debris would require the use of a broom. There was no use defending herself during one of Agnes's tirades. The best course of action was to wait it out in stoic silence.

Mathilda's expression cracked into a smile that didn't

quite reach the vibrant blue eyes. "Now, Agnes. It's not the poor girl's fault that the wind knocked a tree onto the power lines."

So she was a poor girl now, as though she was twelve instead of twenty-seven. Kate kicked a tiny shard of teacup with a bit too much oomph.

Glancing at the disturbance, Mathilda continued. "I'm certain there is a perfectly reasonable explanation as to why Kate is doing the task you specifically assigned to Fiona. Isn't that right, Kate?"

"Yes, ma'am. Fiona isn't feeling well tonight, with the new baby on the way, and I offered to help so she could get off her feet."

"That's kind of you."

"Oh, now, Mathilda, you're being too easy on her," Agnes butted in. She wagged a finger at Kate. "You know good and well that we can't have the likes of you parading in front of the family in your stained chef smock and—" she flicked a grimace at Kate's neck, where Kate could feel the wisps of hair at her nape sticking to her perspiring skin "—common sweat."

There would be no use in pointing out that she was wearing a jacket, not a smock—and a pristine one at that—or that the air-conditioning unit had shut off along with the lights and Kate was perspiring because she'd been standing in an unventilated shaft for nearly ten minutes.

"And you decided, all on your own," Agnes continued, "that you're good enough to serve not just any Colton, but the head of the household?" She hunched her arms around the fresh tray she'd brought with her, hugging it as if Kate's lowly station might taint the precious dish of bread pudding sitting atop it.

This new pudding was from the same batch as the ruined one, but without the whipped cream and whiskey sauce. Agnes had forgotten to add them. Kate squelched a sniff of shock.

From everything Kate knew about Jethro Colton's long list of sins, it was he who wasn't fit to lick her chef clogs, not the other way around. And anyhow, Agnes might think Kate too beneath Mr. Colton's station to serve him like a proper maid, but she would never, *ever,* present him with an incomplete dessert.

She summoned the remnants of her composure. "I thought, with it being so late and with the ranch short on staff, it wouldn't be so bad for me to step in."

Agnes threw an arm up in dramatic disgust. "Wouldn't be so bad? In the name of all things holy, she'll get us all canned."

"Agnes," Mathilda soothed, "of course Kate's face is flushed from working in the heat of the kitchen." She set a supportive hand on Kate's shoulder. "But am I noticing correctly that you changed into a clean smock, dear?"

"A clean jacket, yes, ma'am." Kate's face heated. She loathed being talked down to day in and day out by these women who controlled the flow of life and information at Dead River Ranch. But with no money or family she could turn to, this job was all she had.

At least it came with a well-stocked kitchen to work in and a house of people hungry for sweets.

"As you so astutely pointed out, there's no time to waste," Mathilda continued to Agnes. "If Mr. Colton doesn't get his dessert in short order, we'll all pay the price for the delay. There's no sense in you traipsing up two flights of stairs to Mr. Colton's quarters, not after the scrumptious meals you slaved all day to prepare." Agnes swelled up like a toad at the saccharine compliment. "Allow Kate to do the work."

Well, gee. Thanks. She mashed her lips together and thought about cheesecake. Plain, with a single fresh strawberry sliced on top.

"It would serve you right, Miss High and Mighty. You might as well take over serving Mr. Colton all his meals. If anyone can teach you a lesson about keeping to your rightful place in this house, it would be Jethro Colton."

Mathilda interrupted with a reproachful tsk. "Mind your tone. He's *Mr. Colton* to you."

Agnes's glare cut past Kate and narrowed on Mathilda. "As if you don't know what he's like."

A chorus of chimes, low but distinctive, came through the open ground-level door.

Mathilda gazed at the door, her lips pursed. "What in the world would someone be thinking, intruding on the family at such a late hour?"

"You're not expecting anyone?" Agnes asked.

"Of course not. Mr. Colton needs his rest. I'm afraid our late-night visitor is going to be sorely disappointed.

Excuse me." Holding her long, black skirt out of the way of the spill, Mathilda sidestepped around Agnes's ample form and strode with neat, stiff steps down the stairs and through the door.

"I think I'd like to see who it is, myself." Agnes shoved the dessert tray into Kate's hands. "Go on, now, and hurry up. You think you're too good for kitchen work? Fine. From this point forward, Mr. Colton's meals are your responsibility. Maybe he'll have more mercy on you than he does on the rest of us."

Nothing had ever been handed to Levi Colton except his curse of a name.

Not love or prestige, and definitely not money.

In fact, it was a wonder his fingers retained the dexterity and sensitivity needed of a doctor given the succession of backbreaking jobs he'd toiled through to fight for the life he wanted.

For the hundredth time since he'd driven through the opulent gold-and-white entrance gate to Dead River Ranch, he asked himself the same impossible question he'd been asking the whole drive from Salt Lake City.

What the hell was he thinking, coming here?

The reason had seemed so solid that morning when he'd left his apartment. And it had nothing to do with sympathy for Gabriella, who'd burst into the hospital office he shared with the other first-year residents, with her high-end tailored clothes and porcelain features, begging him to return to Dead River Ranch, insisting that he was the key to her poor, dear father's survival.

Return. As if he'd ever been welcomed there before. As if he would've set a toe on Jethro Colton's property even if he'd been invited. He should've never said "never" because here he was, winding through the ranchland en route to the mansion he'd seen only in pictures.

What the hell was he thinking? Why would he go out of his way, jeopardize his standing at the hospital and place himself in Jethro's line of fire after he'd sworn to never do so again?

"This is my last chance to look into the old man's eyes before he dies," he muttered in reminder as he took a corner too fast. It was the same answer, the only answer, he'd been able to come up with in the seven days since Gabriella ran from his office in tears, proclaiming, "You're a lot like Dad. Stubborn to the end."

The insult hit its mark. Levi had smarted for days at the comparison, stewing about all the many ways he wasn't like Jethro and cursing Gabriella because she'd made him feel something other than indifference for the Coltons, a state of mind Levi worked diligently to maintain.

But for seven straight nights the usual dreams that haunted him were absent, replaced by his mother's image standing beside Gabriella, both of them chanting that he was the spitting image of Jethro. As bad as him, they'd said, sneering. As corrupt and heartless. Time after time he woke drenched in sweat and breathing hard.

Last night, he'd reached his limit. Hating the way the

dreams and subsequent cold sweat made him feel vulnerable, he'd pushed from the bed and taken a shower without turning on the light. The bathroom fixture was too bright for 3:00 a.m., and besides, the darkness was exciting, as if he was bucking the rules. An explorer luxuriating in an underground waterfall.

The whimsy of it almost erased the vision of his mother from his head. But not quite. The knot in his stomach wouldn't completely ease. He braced his hands against the tile, picturing his mother, wondering how accurate his memory of her was or if it had morphed over the years into someone more beautiful, less damaged by the world. He'd have to unearth the box of photographs from storage to know for sure.

Standing there in the dark shower, thinking about her and the unsettling dreams, the eeriest feeling crept through him, as if he sensed the presence of his mother and she was trying to tell him something important.

The problem was, Levi didn't believe in ghosts. He was a doctor, for pity's sake. He didn't buy for one second that his mother had returned from beyond the grave to give him a message that he was the spitting image of the man she'd obsessed over until her dying breath. She'd said that very thing repeatedly while he was growing up, and so the dreams shouldn't have got to him as profoundly as they had. Just random memories surfacing.

Except...

Except he couldn't shake the idea that he needed to prove the lack of resemblance once and for all. He needed to look Jethro in the eye one last time before he died.

Ludicrous because what did he think he'd see in those eyes besides Jethro's typical arrogance and spite? He supposed regret would be too much to hope for from a man who didn't have a soul. Then again, maybe Levi had come back to Wyoming because he knew it would infuriate Jethro to lie there helpless in a sickbed while Levi took charge.

Hadn't that always been a fantasy of his as a little boy—that his father would need him?

Wincing with bitterness at the memory of the naive, hopeful child he'd been, he crested a ridge and the estate and surrounding pastures came into view. Illuminated by the moon, white fences spread in all directions over the rambling land, dividing it into sections for the livestock.

The house itself rose in the center of the spread in grand design, looming over the grounds in absolute darkness. Not a single light was on anywhere around or inside the main house, but only flickers of brightness behind the drawn curtains—candles or flashlights—as though a power line had been cut.

Given the violent wind, it wasn't an outlandish theory that a falling tree had taken out the ranch's power. In the beams of his headlights, leaves danced and skittered across the circular driveway.

He stepped from the car. A gust of warm, foul-smelling summer wind shoved against the side of his body, flipping his shirt collar up and pelting his cheek with bits of dirt.

Those were two things he never missed about Wyoming—
the relentless wind and the odor of livestock.

Folding his collar into place, he studied the house.
Thick, beige stucco walls with rows of identical win-
dows reached up to the sky like a fortress, impenetrable
and impersonal. How could anyone find comfort living in such a monstrosity? A monstrosity for a monster, he supposed.

Gabriella hadn't said if she or either of her two sisters lived here still, but he'd bet they did. He'd bet Jethro
kept his children on short leashes—the bastard son ex-
cluded, of course.

His old friend hatred crawled into his heart. He
loathed that he was still quick to anger about how the
old man had treated Levi and his mother. Because anger
meant he cared. Why couldn't he go numb about the
past like he wanted to? If not numbness, then he'd set-
tle for peace.

Maybe peace would finally come to him when Jethro
succumbed to leukemia.

As he watched from the driveway, the place snapped
into brightness. Floodlights burst to life, illuminating
the driveway in blinding light. Startled, Levi jumped
and gripped the car door. His heart hammering, he
squinted until his eyes adjusted. Faint cheers, women's
voices, erupted on one of the upper floors.

He ducked into the car and popped the trunk, then
hauled out his suitcase and medical bag. There weren't
any hotels he could stomach staying at in the town of
Dead—too many of those bitter memories he hated car-

ing about—and so his only choice besides sleeping in his car was to stay at the ranch. That was, if Jethro allowed him to.

The door was as thick and unwelcoming as the walls. He pushed the doorbell but didn't hear a ring in response. After a few minutes of standing there, second-guessing his choice and asking himself over and over what the hell he was doing there, he raised his fist and knocked.

The door was opened by a severe-looking woman wearing a conservative black dress, her blond hair cut short, utilitarian. "May I help you, sir?"

Levi inhaled deeply. *Here we go....*

A sneaky peek at next month…

INTRIGUE…

BREATHTAKING ROMANTIC SUSPENSE

My wish list for next month's titles…

In stores from 19th July 2013:

❑ Sharpshooter – Cynthia Eden

& Falcon's Run – Aimée Thurlo

❑ The Accused – Jana DeLeon

& Smoky Ridge Curse – Paula Graves

❑ Taking Aim – Elle James

& Ruthless – HelenKay Dimon

Romantic Suspense

❑ Colton by Blood – Melissa Cutler

Available at WHSmith, Tesco, Asda, Eason, Amazon and Apple

Just can't wait?

Visit us Online

You can buy our books online a month before they hit the shops! **www.millsandboon.co.uk**

0713/46

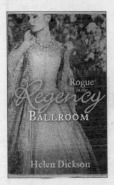
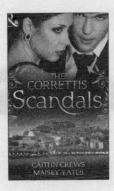

Where will *you* read this summer?

#TeamSun

Join your team this summer.

www.millsandboon.co.uk/sunvshade